Dancing in the Red Snow

DANCING
in the RED SNOW

Sequel to ALMOST PARADISE

ELIZABETH CAIN

DANCING IN THE RED SNOW

This is a work of fiction. All of the characters, names, incidents, organizations, and dialogue in this novel are either the products of the author's imagination or are used fictitiously.

iUniverse books may be ordered through booksellers or by contacting:

iUniverse
1663 Liberty Drive
Bloomington, IN 47403
www.iuniverse.com
1-800-Authors (1-800-288-4677)

Because of the dynamic nature of the Internet, any web addresses or links contained in this book may have changed since publication and may no longer be valid. The views expressed in this work are solely those of the author and do not necessarily reflect the views of the publisher, and the publisher hereby disclaims any responsibility for them.

Any people depicted in stock imagery provided by Thinkstock are models, and such images are being used for illustrative purposes only.
Certain stock imagery © Thinkstock.

ISBN: 978-1-4917-3970-9 (sc)
ISBN: 978-1-4917-3971-6 (hc)
ISBN: 978-1-4917-3969-3 (e)

Library of Congress Control Number: 2014912035

Printed in the United States of America.

iUniverse rev. date: 07/14/2014

I shall find the words I want,
words honed to their essence
by the slow crucifixion of water.

And these words,
divested of edges and anger—
which I shall have found
after plummeting down—

surely, these will be enough for you.

—Joan Raymund

1

◀◀◀◆▶▶▶

The storm broke over the Nevada landscape with senseless slander. Clear, blue summer skies shut down in a devouring gray. Pale-pink bluffs and arroyos turned crimson under the mantle of rain, and lightning started little fires in the mesquite stands. For an hour, no one moved at Rancho del Cielo Azul, seemingly shocked into inaction. Horses screamed in their stalls; the dogs huddled under porches.

Inside the ranch house, Hank Rose sat in the kitchen and looked at his pregnant wife across the oak table his grandfather had made in such a storm decades before. She was trying to eat a bowl of corn chowder but quietly put her spoon down and caught her husband's eyes. He rested one hand over hers and said, "They'll be all right," but his heart was racing. His folks had ridden out before the storm had even shown a particle of itself to bring in some stray cows and calves. Now, they were caught in the violence, somewhere. Julian and Serena Rose knew this country. It had been their home through other conflagrations of terror and grief. Even the storms of Hank's youth they had seen through with grace. What could touch them now?

Susan squeezed her husband's hand. "They'll know what to do," she said. But just as these words came out of her mouth, a distant sound brought them to their feet—the sound of hooves drumming across the desert floor. Hank jammed his arms into his slicker and went out the front door, leaving it banging open in the wind.

The ranch came alive. Julian's greyhounds began barking, and wranglers ran out of the bunkhouse. Someone shouted a greeting to the riders who were still cloaked in heavy mist. The hoofbeats had a desperate rhythm, horses almost out of control seeking the comfort of home. Julian's dappled grey gelding and Serena's shiny Akhal-Teke mare burst into the field next to the barn. A flash from the sky revealed their wet and wounded shapes for a heartbreaking instant. Their saddles were empty.

"Oh God, no!" Hank cried as he grabbed the reins of Paraíso, his mom's mare. The saddle had a deep, black mark on the left fender. The rain had not quite washed the sweat from the horse's scarlet coat. She listed to one side. Some leather straps and a piece of the breast collar had been split by the mare's frantic feet. The foreman, Tyrone, yelled a warning. Hank turned to see his father's horse fall in the red sand and paw at the crackling air around him. A few of the ranch hands somehow wrenched the saddle off of the struggling animal, but he could not stand.

The storm seemed to be moving east, but there was still danger around the edges. The men tacked up their mounts with trembling hands. Hank ordered the women to stay with Susan, who was within a month of her due date, and he came toward her, his horse trotting by his side. "Oh, Henry, please be careful," she said. She was the only one who called him Henry, but it didn't matter what he was called. At that place in the scheme of things, he was just Julian's son, Serena's boy who had always resisted his mother's fearless questioning and teaching but now wanted nothing more than her voice in his ear.

Hank kissed his wife quickly and said, "I'll be back as soon as I can."

He was the last rider out of the yard, galloping to catch the wranglers who were spreading out, searching, calling his mother's and father's names. Thunder inside the lingering storm obliterated the sound of their cries. Hank rode with anguished inner sobs and tears lashing his cheeks, half blinding him. The assaulted land gathered up their horses' hoof steps and swallowed them whole.

An hour passed. Little rivulets had formed in dry ravines. The animals stumbled on the slick, sandstone hills, some horses wearying of the wandering and circling. Billy, one of the boys who'd been on the ranch with Julian since he was eleven, loped up on his burgundy colt. The horse was shaky on his young legs. The now fifty-three-year-old wrangler asked breathlessly, "Hank! What's the last thing they said? Anything. Anything you remember!"

"Just, *We're going to take a short ride. Should be back before the storm rolls in.* That's all," Hank answered, trying to push aside his panic and reason out what might have happened.

Julian and Serena could have gone in any direction. The ranch covered twenty thousand acres, half of it new property that no one had learned the feel of yet. What Hank did know came from his folks' vivid description of the country—the forests of Washoe pine and ponderosa; mirror lakes scattered among towering trees; granite outcrops; acres of hollyhocks and penstemon; columbine and larkspur as high as a stirrup on the creek drainages; and fresh, unblemished grasses for their huge herd of Brahmans.

Can they be there? Hank thought, urging his horse forward. He ached for signs to show him. After a few more miles, the wranglers, his dad's *boys*, as Julian called them, crossed a dry plateau where less rain had fallen, and at last, in a sandy stretch, he saw the hoofprints of the Roses' horses, the distinctive W of the special shoes on his Julian's gelding alongside the fainter marks of Serena's unshod mare.

Hank called out to Tyrone, the foreman who had taught Hank how to ride and had handled ranch guests over the years with skill and patience. "Ty! I'm torn in two here! We have to find my folks pretty soon. I'm afraid to leave Susan for long. It hasn't been a good week for her. But I just keep going farther from the ranch thinking they'll be over the next rise!"

"You go back if you need to," Ty said. "I'm not stopping until I grab Julian's hand and look into Serena's eyes!"

But he couldn't go back. Ahead, riding across the old north boundary, was Henry Dancing Horse, who had befriended Hank when Hank was six and taught him the sacred, Indian way. He reached down in his pocket and touched the Apache Tear, a smooth chunk of black obsidian he had carried with him for twentysome years. Now, it felt as hard and lifeless as his hope.

Then Billy raised his hand. He was still astride his horse on the edge of a deep draw that led into the new territory his folks had named Heaven's Door the day they found it. The first riders who reached that place dismounted, tied their horses to nearby chaparral, and scrambled down into the dark gorge. A cry went up. "We found them!"

Hank reined toward the scene on the rain-soaked desert floor, fear rising in him like the magma of some pent-up volcano. *Oh God, please let them be okay,* he prayed silently. Tyrone grabbed his shoulders and tried to keep him from the sight below. Hank pulled away, climbed down the muddy bank, and went helplessly to his knees where his mother and father lay. They were not breathing, and there was no chance that they ever would. They had done the right thing, curled together in the ditch, holding on, as they always had, to their incandescent love. Hank looked up at the faces lining the hill and shook his head. Then he looked back to the welded bodies and imagined that in the last moment, their love must have flamed up to meet the lightning in its path to earth, the lightning that had extinguished their lives.

Julian had one arm around Serena, his other arm flung at an odd angle and black as the sky above them. Hank's mother was so beautiful at sixty-five, so strikingly real in the shadows of Heaven's Door, he couldn't understand that she would never look at him with her haunting eyes and say, "Hank, my boy, I'll be all right." She didn't look as hurt as Julian, just still, still and silent, as new rain pelted their bodies and the smell of wet burn filled the air.

There was nothing Hank could do. Billy lifted him from the cruel death and got him back on his horse. The last vestige of the storm hovered over the men as they trotted back to the ranch, but here and there, the azure blue of Serena's eyes blazed through the lightning-laced clouds. Two of the boys offered to ride ahead and hitch up the camp wagon, come back, and retrieve the Roses. But as they tightened their horses' girths and prepared themselves for the dreaded task of bearing Julian and Serena out of the drainage, Hank said, with more strength in his voice than he felt, "Don't separate them."

◀◀◀◆▶▶▶

Hank slumped in the saddle and clutched the saddle horn, something he never did, but he felt as if he could fall from the horse at any moment, so deep was his pain. *What will I do without them? They saved me so many times, mostly from my own foolishness,* he thought. They had given him mere suggestions that had turned into huge changes in his life. *Where will those words come from now?* The sky opened to more and more blue, the freak storm gone into another dimension with the souls of Serena and Julian. He pictured his beautiful Iroquois wife with the baby still safe in her womb. His parents would never know their grandchild.

His throat tightened with each step toward home. He had to trust the horse to take him there because he could not stop crying. Henry Dancing Horse had stayed with him, holding his mare back to Hank's slow pace, speaking to him in his Kiowa tongue—words of comfort and sorrow, Hank imagined. The chant-like sound of the Native American's language soothed him and lessened the jarring impact of the deaths and the miles he had to ride from the place where his parents had been struck down.

As the ranch came into view, Hank untied his silk scarf and wiped his face. Susan was waiting for him on the front porch. He knew he didn't have to hide his distress from her. She was a strong woman and still so lovely, one month shy of delivering their child. But he wanted to be strong too, to be able to tell the news without falling apart. He swung off his gelding. Dancing Horse took the reins and turned toward the barn. Hank came slowly up the steps, exhaustion in every move, and took Susan to the swing before he could speak. Then he let the story pour from him.

"They were … struck by lightning. They made it to a huge ditch out by Heaven's Door, but it was too late. One of my dad's arms was … black. His other arm held my mom tight. His head was against hers like maybe he'd been talking to her, maybe saying, 'Hold on, hold on.' She was burned too but not her face. Her face was still … wonderful. Oh God, Susan, it's too terrible to believe."

His wife stroked his back and listened. He released everything he had felt out on the desert.

"What if Mom said to him, 'My only love'? You know how she said that a lot, and Dad smiled as though it had some secret meaning to them. Now we'll never know."

"They were such good people," she said. "Everybody loved them so. And they surely loved each other. Thirty-five years together, weren't they?"

"Yeah … not long enough."

"What will happen now?" she asked.

"Some of the boys have gone with the camp wagon to get them. I have to think what to do. They need to be buried. I don't think I can go through, you know, a funeral and all that. I need to put them in the ground just as they are. I need this to be … over."

"Oh, Henry, I'm so sorry," she said.

That made him smile for a moment. Susan never called him Hank. It had been Henry from the day he met her in college, the lone Native American in his class. He let himself go back to the way they met to distract him from the thought of the wagon carrying his parents to their Rancho del Cielo Azul.

◄◄◄◆►►►

The girl was sitting under a giant cottonwood, book open, head down. He had noticed her before in an art class, but she was out the door quickly at the bell. Her hair was raven black and hung to her narrow waist. Sometimes she braided feathers into a lock or two, sometimes a string of tiny, silver bells. He could hear her coming down the hall and strained to catch a glimpse of her. One day on the quad, he decided to go right up to her and start talking.

"I'm Henry Four Names," he blurted out awkwardly, standing over her. She glanced at him. "You're not Indian," she said.

6

"No," Hank admitted, "but I am a native American."

She laughed then and said, "Well, sit down and tell me all those names."

"Robert Henry Askay Rose. But everybody calls me Hank."

"I'll take Henry," she said pleasantly, and it was Henry from then on. "I'm Susan Sun. I'm here on scholarship. Major—art; minor—music. And now I'm late for a flute lesson." She gathered her books.

Hank held out his hand and helped her to her feet. "Wait," he said. "Where are you from?"

"New Mexico. An orphanage called La Casa de la Paz," she said over her shoulder. She hurried away, tossing her dark hair out of her pretty face.

Hank was sure he was in love.

◄◄◄◆►►►

Now, Hank could barely say a word. He wanted to tell her how incredible her love had been since those college days, how her innocence and shyness had made him feel protective, how her lack of jealousy and possessiveness had healed him of wounds he had suffered in a relationship with a girl in high school named Liana. But he couldn't speak that abusive girl's name in the same sentence with the names of his mother and father who lay dead in each other's arms.

Instead, he thought of the first time he'd kissed Susan.

◄◄◄◆►►►

He had walked her to her dorm after an ice-cream social on campus. They stopped outside. Men weren't allowed in after ten at night. The September wind caressed them. He saw a speck of chocolate on her cheek, bent down, and licked it away. Then their lips came together, and he was hungry for more than chocolate.

"I didn't know you liked that flavor," she said after they finally broke apart.

"I like the flavor of you!" he said. And he kissed her again.

◀◀◀◆▶▶▶

The present startled him back to the rain-chilled and unbearable day. He felt his wife's hand on his arm.

"I see the wagon," Susan said.

The sky had darkened to cobalt. Total darkness would come soon. Hank decided to park the wagon, without moving his folks, somewhere between the ranch house and the barn. He would make a few calls, give people time to come to the ranch if they wanted, and give the wranglers one last night with Julian and Serena. He would bury them the next day at their honeymoon cabin about four miles away in a spring-fed canyon where trees and wildflowers burst in lush profusion from the desert floor.

When he finally found his voice and told Susan this, she said, "I think that would honor them in a fine way."

So Hank left her for a short time to direct Billy, who drove the horse-drawn wagon into the yard, to the place he had chosen. Ranch hands and staff emerged from the bunkhouse and the kitchen. Some held back; some went right up to see the bodies before they could believe such a thing had happened. Henry Dancing Horse began circling the wagon with Nevada sage burning in a shell, blowing the smoke over Serena and Julian. Hank knew this was done to purify the space in which his parents embraced in their blackened shells, but it was ironic to him too because it was fire that had killed them and smoke that had risen from their remains before they were ever found.

Tyrone brought Askay, the Roses' Tanzanian cook and long-time companion, out to the circle of sorrow. He pushed the old man's wheelchair right up to the wagon. Askay was ninety-one and failing, but he placed his hands on the wooden railings and pulled himself to his feet. "I stand for you, Julian, my beloved Julian, and for Serena, my angel, Serena. I give you last tie to earth, my last black rose." He reached through the railings and placed the rose next to their welded bodies, already black and headed for the dark earth. Ty helped the aging African back into the chair but told him he could stay there as long as he wished. He bowed his head. Askay was a Catholic and had more prayers to say than anyone, more beliefs about where the Roses might go to be with God. He sat in the Kiowa smoke, his rosary sparkling in the last rays of sunlight fading from the sky.

Hank could not look again, but Susan climbed into the wagon and kissed each one, translating for her husband the words of her Iroquois blessing. He was so amazed that she could touch the damaged flesh.

"Henry," she said, "do you want the rings?"

He didn't want to think about that but finally whispered, "Just the diamonds. Leave the wedding bands." He reached out to help his wife down. Then she placed in his hand his mother's white diamond surrounded by a heart of black diamonds. "You are healing me already," he said.

Darkness fell around them and the mourners in the yard. Ty rolled Askay back to his room in the main house. Angie, one of the women who had worked for Julian before Serena came to the ranch, had been making phone calls and now walked over from her cabin, tears fresh on her face.

"Oh Hank, this is just awful," she said. "I remember the day your mom showed up here looking for work. I believe your dad fell in love with her the first time he saw her in the round pen with a troubled horse. I've called a lot of their friends. Please tell me what else I can do."

"Thanks, Angie," he said. "I'll need some time for sure. Could you keep an eye on Susan if I get sidetracked by ... things?"

"Sure," she said.

Susan jumped in. "I'll be okay, Henry, as long as you are." But Hank asked Angie to take her arm on the way back to the house so his wife wouldn't stumble on the path.

Hank leaned against Dancing Horse, who had paused in his smudging ceremony. The Native American said, "They will always be with me," nodding at the still figures of his patrons. "They loved me when I was just a defiant Indian kid from the Res. How many people do that? Yeah, I could ride, but your mom taught me how to be *with* the horse. It changed my life."

"And you changed mine," Hank said. "It's kind of a circle." He drew his hands through the air around the scene. "Like this."

"A little bit broken, hey?"

"A little bit broken."

◄◄◄◆►►►

In the morning, Tyrone hitched Julian's matching chestnut Belgians to the wagon, with Julian and Serena now covered with a quilt made by Askay's family and brought from Africa when he first joined the ranch staff for Julian's parents, Helen and Henry Rose. "Please wrap around them when taken from wagon ... so earth not see what lightning has done," he said.

The foreman drove the horses slowly down to the gate under the sign Rancho del Cielo Azul. But the sky was not blue. It threatened to rain again on the line of cars and trucks beginning to form on the local road that crossed by the ranch entrance just before it turned onto the main highway south toward Elko. Hank was on his grey gelding, brother to Julian's grey that still had not gotten up from where he fell by the barn the day before. The horse was being tended to by ranch hands supervised by Dancing Horse with his Native methods of ministering to wounded animals, but it didn't look good.

Hank could not abide the thought of burying that gorgeous and sensitive animal the same day he buried Julian, so he chose to ride, to honor his father and his father's suffering horse. He trotted back and forth along the procession. Arms reached out to touch him, grab his hand, and speak some words of sympathy. Hank liked the motion of the grey and could canter away from his folks' grieving friends when he had to.

Susan rode in the first truck with Billy and Askay. The other wranglers fit their vehicles into the line as it began its solemn trek across the hard, desert ground to the mile-long, narrow horse trail to the old honeymoon cabin. Mourners would have to hike from there. All could not go but would toss flowers and mementos into the wagon with its shocking load.

There was no coffin. There was no pastor. There was only the bitter wind and the sound of weeping to accompany Julian and Serena in their stunning embrace to the place they would merge into the earth with the black rose. The ones who made it to the cabin might have heard in their minds the music of "Almost Paradise," the song the Roses danced to many Saturday nights, surprising everyone who saw in them, even from the first night, a startling passion. The watchers then at the grave might have thought of Julian and Serena sharing their last dance. Aspens and evergreens swayed along the creek in a dance of their own in an oasis of rich life guarding the dead parents of Robert Henry Askay Rose.

2

◀◀◀◆▶▶▶

Three weeks after the burial of Julian and Serena, Susan Rose delivered a black-haired, almond-eyed girl she and Hank named Marta Serena Sun Rose, but the girl would be called Sunny for her bright temperament, which revealed itself almost immediately. It didn't take much to make her smile, and she seemed happy, even in the arms of strangers. When Susan was tired, the baby was willing to be put down somewhere and sleep peacefully even with the sharp sounds of ranch life around her.

Askay was honorary grandfather and did his share of holding the girl so Susan could keep up with her regular chores and have some valuable time with her husband in his time of grief. Hank carried Sunny around the yard and out to the barn, introducing her to dogs and horses as well as the humans who lived and worked on the ranch. If Susan felt like it, she hooked her arm through one of Hank's and walked with them, naming things for the child in her Iroquois tongue. Hank repeated the words in Spanish, and later, in the house, Askay renamed *love* and *blessing* and *rain* in Swahili. Hank seemed to think the first thing Sunny said sometime in her first six months of life was some form of *mvua*, which was Swahili for rain. His joy at hearing his daughter's first word lifted him from the pain of the day the thunderstorm had swept his parents, her grandparents, out of their lives.

Hank found peace in the daily routines with Sunny, his loving wife, and ranch duties. But there were surprises. A few weeks after Sunny was born, Hank was on his way out the door to check on his mother's horse. The Akhal-Teke mare seemed to be languishing, barely eating whatever was offered to her, and moving with an unbalanced gait. The phone rang as he opened the front door, so he stepped back into the kitchen and answered brusquely, "What?"

"Hank?"

"Yeah?"

"This is Carla," a voice said with some emotion. "Serena's friend … trainer."

"Oh."

"No one told me about … what happened," she said. "I had to read it in the paper."

"We didn't call everyone. We wanted it over, ma'am."

"But I was special to her," she said.

"Ma'am, everyone was special to her," Hank said wearily.

"No, you don't understand. We loved each other. We had a *relationship*."

"That's not possible," Hank said.

"She never told you?"

"You gave her dressage lessons. What else was there to know?"

"We were in love. I should have been there," she said.

Hank sat down heavily in the nearest chair. "What? That's crazy! My mother only loved my father. They're together forever now."

"A part of me is with her too. I need to see where she is."

Hank hesitated. He just wanted to get rid of this woman. "Ma'am, we've decided to close that area to family only. I'm sorry."

"This isn't over," she said and hung up.

Hank went out to the barn, his head reeling from the confrontation with the woman Carla. His mother could have explained this. She'd never lie to him. But did he really want to know? He found Billy rubbing Serena's mare with liniment that Dancing Horse had made. *Mom had lessons on this horse with Carla. Sometimes she rode out on the trail for hours with the woman. Could she have … loved her like … it might be true,* Hank thought.

He blurted out, "Billy, what do you know about Carla and my mom?"

Billy looked up from the flank of the mare, and something changed in his eyes. "Hank, all that was a long time ago. It doesn't matter now."

"It matters to me," Hank said.

"Some things should go to the grave."

"Not *this*, Billy. Please."

"All right. When your mother first came here, she told me she'd been in a relationship and wasn't looking for another. A couple of weeks later, I watched Julian take her in his arms for a dance. There was no question who she loved then."

"But before? She loved a *woman*?" Hank asked.

"I finally figured that out, but Carla was never a threat to your folks' relationship."

"She seems a threat now," Hank said. "To my peace of mind."

"How?"

"She wants to see where Serena's buried."

"Hank, you have to ask yourself, what would Serena want?"

Hank thought of the day his mom visited the principal when he was in second grade and demanded that her son be allowed to use his Native American name. If she had ever loved the woman, she'd want him to be generous. *My mother is still showing me the way,* he thought. *Carla standing at her grave is closing the circle a little more. It's what she'd want.* Hank mixed some special feed for his mom's mare. He dreaded knowing about the women's relationship. Relationships in his family had taken some tragic turns, but Julian and Serena had faced them head on. Now, he must learn to do that.

Sunny was the highlight of his life. He must save his energy for being her dad, for keeping her safe. A shiver went through him. The world held dangerous places—the cliffs where his grandparents went down in their small plane, the edge of Heaven's Door where his parents were struck by lightning. He spoke some words of comfort to the horse, the only survivor of *that* danger, and walked over to the tack room door where his mom and dad had hung his grandmother's watercolor—a captivating painting of a scared horse in a round pen surrounded by grim-faced cowboys with spurs and whips. He always looked at that part first. Then his eyes sought the redeeming piece of the old picture—his grandmother's arm reaching through the rails with a gift for the bronc. That part always made him cry, especially now that his father, her son, was gone. He took it off the door and returned to the main house with the thought, *Yes, even my grandmother knew to offer love first, so that's what I'll do with Carla.*

◄◄◄◆►►►

Susan had made dinner with Askay giving her instructions from his wheelchair. Sunny was already in her crib, which had been Hank's crib and his father's before that. Askay ate a few bites as if testing to see if Susan had done it right and then excused himself. His grandson, Akmal Joseph, who had been so loyal to Julian and Serena as they aged, had gone back to Africa just a few months ago. The young man still did not know about the Roses' deaths or Sunny's birth, but his own family needed him now in Arusha, with crushing poverty keeping his brothers and sisters from going to school. Hank noticed that Askay had seemed to decline after Akmal left, no chance now for him to return to the land of his birth or to be buried where the Southern Cross dazzles the sky below the equator, a constellation Askay searched for when he first arrived in America, not understanding yet that he would never see it again.

Hank always missed Askay when he didn't stay at the table. For years he had cooked the most incredible meals, concocted tribal medicines from herbs and barks that somehow made it through the mail from Tanzania to the ranch in the isolated northeast of Nevada, and defended Julian and Serena's love when it seemed the impossible, maybe even improper, thing. This Hank's mother had told him but didn't elaborate on what might have been proper or not. He knew his folks had fallen in love while his father was still married, but perhaps Askay knew some deeper truths. *Does the old man know about Carla? Did he discover enough about it to reveal more to me than Billy did or than Carla herself might?* Hank mused as he tasted the exquisite blend of rice, bananas, cucumbers, mint, cilantro, and lime.

It was quiet in the kitchen as Hank and Susan sat at the oak table where his folks had explained the existence of his dad's ex-wife, locked in a mental institution for unthinkable crimes, long before he'd met Susan or believed such craziness could happen. So some secrets he knew. The one about his mother and Carla baffled him. He picked at his food, though it was delicious. Susan stopped eating and caressed his arm.

"Aren't you feeling well, Henry?" she asked.

"I'm okay, honey. I just found out something about my mother, and it's bothering me," he said.

"What is it?"

"Do you know who Carla is?"

She hesitated just enough for him to realize she knew more than he did about the subject.

"I shouldn't know this," she said, "but I heard something once that I felt I shouldn't repeat. I thought I should keep your mother's words private. Don't you?"

"She loved a woman. I get it."

"No, no, Henry, you don't!"

"I *want* to get it, but it's a mystery to me. I want to understand how a woman could love a woman … *that* way," he said.

"I don't know if I even understand that. But I believe your mother would have told you. So I hope I'm doing the right thing." She took a deep breath and went on. "One day last year, I passed by the tack room. The door was slightly open, and I saw your mother pull away from Carla. And Carla said, 'Why can't you love me again? I'll never love anyone else like I love you.' Then Serena said, 'Julian is my life, my only love. Please care for me for who I really am.' I thought it was the loveliest rejection I'd ever heard. I didn't imagine it would ever come up again."

"Well, Carla called me today."

"Really?"

"She wants to know where Serena is buried."

"What are you going to do?"

"I'm going to give her the closure she needs. It's the right thing."

"Henry, you are so like your father, generous and good."

"I'll show you how generous I can be," he said, nodding toward the bedroom.

Her eyes sparkled. "We can't wake the baby."

"I can be generous *and* quiet," he teased.

"Okay, you're on," she said.

He laughed and cuddled her on their way to their gold-hued, silk-outfitted bed.

◄◄◄◆►►►

In the morning, Hank looked through Serena's address book and found Carla's number. He listened to the answering machine and gathered his courage to say, "Carla, this is Hank Rose. I'll be glad to take you to my folks' gravesite. Anyone who loved my mother deserves that, at least. We'll have to ride. Bring your English saddle. Oh, maybe you can help with my mom's horse. I think the mare needs a feminine touch. And forgive my—" The machine cut off, apparently full.

This last idea had just come to him as he spoke into the recorder. Why not let Carla feel useful. God knows they'd tried everything with the horse. Carla was a skilled horsewoman; he had to give her that. But he wasn't sure how he'd feel when he came face to face with a woman who had wanted to take his mother's love from his father.

Carla called the next day. "Hank, thank you. I know this is hard for you. It's just that ... I need to say good-bye."

"I could use your help with Mom's mare. She was hit by the lightning too and is very weak on one side ... and maybe has kind of given up," Hank told her.

"Oh, I'd love to take care of Paraíso! What about your dad's horse?"

"He didn't make it."

"I'm so sorry ... about everything. I'll drive out tomorrow if that's okay."

"Yeah. I'll be here."

They hung up. Susan was feeding the baby. Hank watched with awe, sad that his mother would never see this engaging scene. "I'm gonna take Carla up to the canyon tomorrow," he said.

"That's good, Henry."

◄◄◄◆►►►

Carla appeared late the following morning, saddle in hand. Hank met her with two horses, one a nice dressage horse that was good on the trail. "We might as well head out," Hank said. "It may storm today."

"Fine with me," she said.

It was an early August day but cold and blustery. The horses were restless. They could have taken the truck nearly all the way to the cabin, but Julian and Serena had almost always ridden, so it felt right to do it that way. They didn't speak for a while. There was a hawk making whistling sounds high above and the comforting clomp of horse hooves on hard sand. If a storm did come, it would bring unseasonable snow, Hank was sure. The graves and his heart would be covered with ice in the middle of summer.

Carla finally said, "I knew about this place, but Serena never brought me here."

Hank didn't respond.

She went on, "I tried to understand how she could love Julian. Even on their wedding day, I thought she was making a mistake, as beautiful as they were together."

"I guess it wasn't a mistake, ma'am," Hank had to say.

"I know. I was the one who made the mistake."

"Ma'am?"

"I let her go."

"She made her choices. I think we should leave it at that," Hank said.

They were in the canyon now. The red sandstone walls towered over them. The hoof steps had an echo. The sky darkened. The grave was behind the house, up the trail a ways.

"Carla." He felt funny saying her name. "I'll take the horses and go back to the cabin, leave you a bit."

She dismounted and handed him the reins, but before Hank turned, he saw her place a locket on a silver chain over the gravestone. He glanced at the words carved in the marble, the headstone that Billy had brought up some days after the burial. It read: *We took our blessings from all who would give them and thank God we are on the last trail together.*

He felt his throat closing up, so he led the horses down toward the old house and gave Carla the time she needed. Whatever had been between this woman and his mother would fade now with the desert verbena and the roses from Askay's garden that had been laid there. *Who am I to judge someone else's love?* he thought.

Carla didn't stay too long. Soon she was coming down the trail toward him. *What could she say to the silent earth and to someone wrapped in another's arms?* Hank reasoned as they began to wind their way out of the canyon. A hawk that lived there escorted them, screeching and diving on the wind. When they reached the ranch, Carla said abruptly, "I won't be coming back. I have to let everything go now. I hope I wasn't too much trouble."

"No, ma'am."

"I don't think I can be around Paraíso right now. Too many memories. But let me know how she does, all right?"

"I will," Hank said.

He stood in the driveway holding the two horses and watched her pull away from the ranch. She hadn't asked to see the baby, but Hank thought of the years to come with his daughter. Would he have to worry constantly about her choice of friends, her dreams, the experiences that may not be what he wanted for her? And Susan would have her own deep concerns and guarding ways. *Oh man, how Julian and Serena must have despaired over my relationship with that wild Liana when I was a teenager. Will Susan and I have the strength to fight Sunny's battles? Will she want us to?*

In the week following Carla's brief visit, Hank wandered on horseback around the riding loops his mother and father and his grandparents before that had created for paying guests, his mind seeking a definition for *his* family. There were roping and dressage clinics scheduled, some round pen work Angie and Ty had promised to do for folks with unpredictable horses. Serena had started that program years ago, and it was hard to just close it down. Julian had still owned a thousand head of cattle. How could he fit all these things in with his responsibilities as a father?

Most of his dad's wranglers were in their sixties and had slowed down some. Henry Dancing Horse and Billy were younger, but their lives were complicated. Dancing Horse and his wife, Willow, had a daughter who would be a senior in high school that year. Rachel Endless Rain, as they had named her when she was born during the wettest year on record in Nevada, was active in track and drama. Her activities could easily take her parents away from the ranch at times Hank needed them the most—for roundups, on branding and doctoring days, or for checking fences. Billy was seeing a gal in Elko and hit the road as soon as his chores were done. Hank was overwhelmed by the way things had changed after one damn storm!

Serena's mare, Paraíso, named in honor of Hank's German shepherd that Liana had killed in a fit of jealousy, seemed to be getting better without Carla's magic, but Hank felt lost. Susan had her hands full with baby Sunny, but she didn't ask for his help much. Probably some Iroquois pride, Hank reasoned. And she had Luz, Marta's grandniece, to give her a break if she wanted it. Marta was gone now, had a stroke that killed her while she hung clothes on the line during a power outage. She had been brought from Mexico by Hank's grandparents, Helen and Henry, even before Julian was born. She had lived in the main house and taken care of everything from housekeeping to bookkeeping. She and Askay had a friendly competition with the cooking. Whose dishes would delight the family the most—African or Mexican? Hank missed those days.

One day in the first part of September, Hank went out and sat in the round pen, in the exact spot where he was born. He tried to imagine his mother's pain and surprise that he was so eager to arrive in the world that there was no time to get to the hospital. Right there in the ring's sand, Serena had been slammed to the ground, her labor coming hard and fast. Serena, who might have loved a woman but chose his father and gave him life. Hank didn't pray much, but at that moment, he asked whatever God might hear him to keep Julian and Serena in a state of grace.

He remembered his mother telling him how the local Catholic priest had blessed them the night before she married Julian, on a Christmas Eve, asking God for peace and grace for them, even though they weren't of his faith. Hank pounded the earth with his fists and cried out to that same God in a dark rage, "They were so beautiful! How could you let them die! We are all diminished!" Then he let the anger go.

◄◄◄◆►►►

"Where have you been, Henry?" Susan asked as he came through the door.

"I was in the round pen," he said.

"Oh."

"I'm okay now. I had to ask God something," Hank said.

"You don't talk to God."

"I do now," he said, surprising himself.

"Well, I think that's okay. Will you tell me what he says?"

He smiled. "Sure."

The Iroquois were so literal. But Hank had to consider that his wife was raised in a Christian orphanage. She had explained to him early in their relationship that she was not exactly abandoned by her relatives, who were descendants of early Iroquoian peoples from the northeast. Her mother had died in a fire, and her father thought Susan could be better educated in a respectable, religious institution in New Mexico. Hank still couldn't figure that one out. Would he do such a thing for Sunny? Or would he let her find her own way, to God or not? Right then he knew he would not want to be separated from his daughter for any reason.

Sunny fussed in her crib, so Susan left him with a quick hug and went to tend to their child. The wind had begun to whirl outside. Cold air found the cracks in the chinking, and Hank was glad that most of the outdoor clinics were behind them. Folks had been asking Dancing Horse to teach a session on the historical Indian way of riding with only a thin rope in the horse's mouth. Eleven people had signed up, most of whom had seen the remarkable ride the Native American had done on Serena's warmblood years ago when they were kids themselves, dressage sans saddle and bridle. The indoor arena would make that clinic possible even with rain threatening outside. Hank set a date in the third week of September.

The ranch began to find its normal fall rhythm. Horses got broke, the garden mulched, and firewood stacked in the main house, bunk house, and guest cabins. Snow fleetingly pelted the ground, and the temperature dropped. Billy and Tyrone drove the tractors that unrolled the round hay bales for the cattle that had been brought in from the range. The farrier pulled shoes, and some of the horses got blanketed at night. Hank felt a small satisfaction that things were running smoothly, although a certain joy was gone.

Late one day, after a long, cold ride to find some wayward cattle, Hank walked into the kitchen and saw Sunny in Susan's arms. The sight of those two precious girls always made his heart beat faster. Their dark hair and almond-shaped eyes reminded him of paintings he'd seen in Western museums, the strong bond between Native American mothers and their children shining out of the canvases, now transformed to his own rooms. The two together, his wife and daughter, seemed like such a reliable thing, and some of his doubts about the future vanished.

Would his daughter hold the key to Heaven's Door? That remarkable, unexplored territory that had been Julian and Serena's dream? He thought of that line from "Almost Paradise," the song that was so special to his folks. Now, that paradise was his to discover, his to maintain. His to leave for Sunny, as Julian had left it for him.

Luz came in from Askay's room and said that the Tanzanian wanted to see him. Hank knew his new peace would be dampened by the sight of the old man wasting away, but he went down the hall to the last room, the quietest place in the ranch house, where the windows looked out on distant peaks rising over ten thousand feet. Askay was in the wheelchair by his bed and one of the nightstands. He beckoned to Hank and then grasped his hands.

"My Julian's son," he said softly.

"*Habari za jioni?* How are you doing tonight?" Hank greeted him in his language.

"I ... be fine, young Hank." He released Hank's hands and picked up a thick, worn leather volume from the nearby table. His arms seemed to struggle with the weight of the book. "This for you."

"What is it?"

"My words, from when your grandfather brought me to ranch. Many years. Many years. Things you should know. Things you should remember. Words of paradise. Some things not easy to write, not easy to read. You will understand."

"Maybe I'm not ready for this," Hank said.

"You be ready, son," the African responded. "I saw your mama's round pen birth you. I watched you grow. I saw your heart stray. I saw your father snatch you out of much trouble. These things remain when spirit is uncertain. Trust it. I not always be here to ... to help you," he continued shakily.

Hank took the journal, realizing suddenly that this meant Askay did not mean to, or could not, write in it anymore.

"But, Askay, what if I have questions? I didn't always listen to my dad or especially my mom. When he was branding calves, I was running on some track far away. When Serena was refining a half-pass, I was making a pass at a demented older girl. What do I know?"

"Hank Rose ... answers ... in your blood," he said.

"And now ... in Sunny's blood," Hank said.

The old man closed his eyes.

"Are you tired now?" Hank asked.

"Yes ... but stay a while ... and then, bring me baby girl. African blessing may follow her wherever she goes if I cannot."

Later that evening, Hank put Sunny in Askay's arm. The girl reached up and touched his wrinkled, black face.

"Ah," Askay said. "Old life and new life. Which can give most to the other?" And he whispered some words in Swahili that Hank wasn't sure of. Would they be enough? When might his daughter ask a question that only Askay could answer?

◀◀◆▶▶

But when winter finally settled in, branding the land with a shroud of white and bitter winds that scoured roads and trees and the beautiful garden, darkening the skies by four o'clock, and startling the ravens and coyotes to silence, Askay died.

The African did not wake one morning from a solemn sleep. Hank's grief was doubled, as Askay had been like a father to him, listening to his childhood fantasies, letting him follow him around in the kitchen, letting him cry when his first puppy died, something he would not do in front of Julian. As a teen, when he would sneak off in Julian's truck and come home to his dad's anger, Askay would take him aside and say, "Remember, some day you be father."

Now, those words were so powerful for Hank because he couldn't imagine being angry with Sunny. He would read the old man's thick diary and find the wisdom he needed to raise his child. Susan brought the baby to him just then and said, "Life goes on, Henry."

"But she'll never know Askay," he said. "I need him to be here for her."

"Now, she needs *you*," Susan said quietly.

A few days later, they buried Askay next to Julian and Serena at the canyon house. They had to build a great fire over the gravesite to thaw the ground. The snow turned red with hot coals whipped by the breeze. The coals burned and tumbled upon one another, unmindful of the silent couple dancing below. Hank could not stay too long there. Everything was too fresh—his heart pounding, his head spinning with the image of his mother and father trying to hide from the lightning.

"*Kwa heri*," he said in the African's tongue and then, in a voice he wasn't sure could ever speak again, "Good-bye."

◀◀◀◆▶▶▶

Thus, the baby Sunny spent her first year enveloped in her parents' sadness. She seemed aware of their sorrow somehow and didn't cry or make the usual infant demands. The girl knew the nickers of the horses, the yips and howls of the ranch dogs and desert coyotes more than the sound of Hank's or Susan's voice. She seemed to be honoring them with her quiet ways. Susan said it was just her Indian blood, that generations of Native Americans had taught their children not to cry, not to give away their presence to the enemy. Hank knew that scientifically the theory of acquired characteristics was inaccurate, but he liked that Sunny knew how to hide her voice from the enemy of grief.

3

◀◀◀◆▶▶▶

Just before Sunny's first birthday, on the anniversary of her grandparents' death, a summer storm broke across Rancho del Cielo Azul. The wranglers had planned a ride to the burial site by the old cabin but instead gathered around the grave of Julian's dappled grey horse, their yellow slickers the only bright mark on the landscape. Susan held her little girl and watched from the ranch house window as Hank walked out toward the somber group. Rain pelted the glass. Sunny twirled her hands in her mother's raven hair.

It took a while for things to seem normal after that. The summer was edged with cloudbursts and silences, the fall and winter colder and whiter than anyone remembered. Even the fair closed early when two feet of snow fell in October. On Christmas Day, Hank reached across the dinner table and took Susan's hand.

"I don't know if I can talk about Julian and Serena until I have to explain what happened to them to our daughter," he said.

"You have to follow your heart, Henry."

"Yeah, but I can hardly bear to think that my folks and our child will never know each other."

"She's part of them. You'll find the right words," Susan said and squeezed his hand.

As spring nudged at the dark wall of Sunny's second year, and she cried, "Name! Name!" at the budding heads of the purple crocus, Hank felt the words form inside him like the strong bulbs that pushed through the lingering snow. He would tell her everything about her grandparents, their way with horses, their deep passion for each other and the land, their struggle with Miranda, his dad's ex-wife, and even the way they had died in the electric storm, but he would not tell her the exact day of their passing. She might hear it from someone or figure it out, but he would not put in the same sentence the words of joy at her birth with the scarring sorrow he had felt at his loss three weeks before. No. She would never be made to believe that she came along just to save him and Susan from grief. He would separate her birth from that death as long as he could.

When the second anniversary of the Roses' death came at the end of June, the sky was bluer than Serena's eyes, and the sky begged its own clouds to stay away. The day seemed more like a celebration than a mourning. Wranglers paused in their work and whispered some words to Hank, reminding him of an adventure or a lesson they had learned from Serena or Julian. It was getting easier for Hank to hear those words.

On Sunny's second birthday, a man came up the ranch house steps with his hat in his hands. He was vaguely handsome, clean-shaven, and well-dressed. Hank opened the door expecting a nearby rancher or maybe a lawyer from town.

"Hank Rose?" the man asked.

"Yes."

"Sorry to just show up like this, but I'm your uncle Jason … Julian's brother," the stranger said.

Hank's mouth fell open. He had never heard of this man.

"May I come in?" He bowed to Susan as she approached with Sunny in her arms. "Ma'am," he said.

"How do we know …" Hank began, but the man was prepared, holding out a photo of two young men in their twenties, arm in arm. It was unmistakably Julian and the stranger at the door.

"I can explain," Jason said.

"Okay," Hank said. "Come in then."

They all sat in the living room. Luz brought in tea, sodas, and cookies. There was an awkward silence, and then Jason burst right in. "I've waited way too long. I've missed so much. I left my brother and his lovely wife on their wedding day. I got busy up in Montana, logging and packing in hunters. I was rarely by a telephone in those days, but that's no excuse. I loved my brother. Now, here you are, my nephew, all grown up and with a beautiful child. Oh, I'm so sorry," he said. He put his head in his hands, like Hank had seen Julian do so often.

"I believe you're my uncle," Hank said, "but I don't know how I can help you."

"Will you let me be in your life, get to know you both and your little girl?"

Sunny answered that question by suddenly stretching her arms out to the man and saying, "Are you my birthday present?"

Hank and Susan laughed, and Jason cried. They gave him Askay's old room and didn't pressure him to reveal why he had stayed away all these years. He pitched right in to help with chores and rode the kinks out of some rough horses. He was an intelligent and insightful horseman, but he complied with the *boys* who had ridden for his brother and Serena, letting them make the rules, which Hank especially appreciated.

Jason and Hank stayed up late night after night, turning slowly the pages of photo albums, Hank having to stop on almost every page to describe some event in the Roses' lives. They started with the present and moved back along the threads of the years that had tied the family together without Jason. Finally, after his uncle had been on the ranch about a month, they came to Julian and Serena's wedding day, the bride so young and bright next to her husband, just as beautiful in his own way. Jason placed his hand over the picture and looked at Hank. "I will see it," he said, "but I want to tell you … that was the day I walked out."

"Why?" Hank asked, startled by his uncle's move to cover the photo.

"She's wearing your grandmother's wedding dress. I couldn't bear it then. Our mother had only died that year, and here was Julian standing next to someone I didn't know in *her* dress. I thought all kinds of paranoid things, that Serena was only after my brother's money, or that she was trying to take Mom's place in his affection, to cut me out. Of course, if I had stayed, I might have seen a wholly different Serena."

"She was the best thing that ever happened to him," Hank said.

"So that is what I will find," he said, removing his hand.

Jason studied the photograph for a long time. It was the one where they had turned to face the guests as man and wife. Julian's brother was already on the road back to Montana by then.

"Oh, how perfect they look together. How could I have been so foolish?" Jason exclaimed.

"We all do foolish things," Hank admitted, thinking of his teenage years and the name he had not spoken aloud since.

"I think I'll sleep on *this* one," Jason said. "Will you tell me more?"

"All I can," Hank promised, knowing there were some things he would never tell.

Later that week, when his uncle asked whatever happened to Miranda, his brother's mentally-ill first wife, Hank just said, "She died."

Hank didn't hold Jason's estrangement from Julian and Serena against him. It had been a terrible misunderstanding, and neither brother had known how to make the first move after that. Jason asked Hank over and over to tell him stories about Serena so he could love her for all the years he'd mistrusted her. The old man cried when he heard how she revived the minds of horses in the round pen, rewarding the slightest changes toward acceptable and safe behavior, how she adored Julian and seemed to favor him over Hank himself.

"One time, Dad and I were both sick from some bad food we'd eaten in town," Hank began. "I think I was only about ten. My mother would not leave Julian's side for an instant. I was turned over to Marta and Askay. I probably got the best deal because those two had their Mexican and African remedies to help me, but my dad got Serena. It was always like that."

"It pleases me so much to know that's the kind of woman she was," Jason said. "Poor, little sick boys aside." He laughed.

Hank loved sharing these scenes and memories from his youth and beyond. It seemed to be bringing the brothers back together somehow. Yet he could see another death looming. Jason was eighty-one. He didn't look it, and he seemed healthy, but he'd been alone for years and had a melancholy air about him. Hank was already thinking of ways to prepare Sunny for the loss of her granduncle.

But that year, having his father's brother there seemed like a gift from God. Hank was uncomfortable thinking about God and always deferred to his wife's Great Spirit. But this reunion with his uncle took some of the edge off of losing his folks and almost felt like a divine blessing. He was even able to ride with Jason out to the boundary of Heaven's Door and search along the gullies and washes for the place Julian and Serena had died. He might not have been able to find it except that the wranglers had marked it with crosses and rosaries and eagle feathers, the horseshoes from Julian's grey and Serena's lariat, the one she always used in the round pen.

A late spring storm rolled over, reminding them of the fragility of breath and life, and they loped back to the safety of the ranch, bonded in a new way.

◄◄◄◆►►►

By the time Sunny was three, she and Jason were great friends to the delight of Hank. His uncle carried her on his shoulders around the barn, where she could call out all the names of the horses. She called Julian's brother Jase and asked him to tell her about growing up with his brother, the grandfather she never knew. When Jason tired, she slipped from his arms and let him go back to the easy chair in the house.

One time, he showed her the photographs. When they came to the one of Julian and Serena on their wedding day, she piped up in a clear voice, "I'm going to wear that dress when I get married."

"Well, won't you look like a princess," her uncle said.

"I don't want to be a princess," she replied. "I want to be *her*," she went on, putting a small finger on the figure of Serena in white. Of course, her skin was darker, her eyes that striking, almost almond shape.

Jason laughed. "Honey, I don't think you're ever going to look like that!"

Sunny said, "No. I don't mean to *look* like her. I mean to be ... *inside* her."

Hank had just walked into the room and heard his daughter. "I think you have a lot to learn before that, sweetheart!" he said.

In Hank's mind, Jason had the patience of a saint. He stood in the round pen almost every day, helping Sunny with her dappled grey 14.3 hand gelding, which had the shape and face of her favorite stuffed toy. She hadn't named either of them, so her uncle told her that her grandfather's favorite horse was just called Grey, which Hank had told him one day with the album, turning to a photograph of Julian mastering a half-pass on his big-moving grey gelding.

"Okay, mine will be Grey Boy," Sunny said.

That year, Hank only let her walk her little horse with Jason by her side. She wouldn't let anyone lead her. She insisted on holding the reins and trying to fit her legs into the western stirrups. But when Hank found a child's English saddle and punched holes in the leathers until the stirrups would be short enough for Sunny, he asked which way she wanted to learn first.

"How did Grandma Serena ride?" she asked.

"She liked English best," he answered.

"Then that's what I want!" Sunny said.

She got so good on Grey Boy the summer she turned four, with her natural affinity for all things equine, that Hank thought about entering her in the Little Tots riding class that fall at the fair, but Susan wouldn't hear of it.

"I didn't ride unsupervised until I was five," she reasoned.

"I rode at four," Hank said.

"You were a *boy*!" she snapped. "Forget it, Henry. I'm not letting her!"

Hank acquiesced but longed for the moment his daughter would follow the tradition of winning horsewomen in his family. He finally got Susan to agree she could go with them to the fair that year, because Dancing Horse's daughter, Rachel, was riding in the Indian races.

Hank said to Sunny, who was listening intently, "I met Dancing Horse at the Indian Races when I was six. We had the same first name—Henry."

"What Momma calls you," she said.

"Yeah. Anyway, I yelled and screamed for Dancing Horse, and he won! He liked me from then on, called me Henry Four Names."

"Am I an Indian?" Sunny asked.

"You are half native American and half Native American."

She sighed and said, "Daaa-dy! What does *that* mean?"

But he wanted to put off the answer, knowing he would have to explain it before she started school. There was so much she couldn't understand yet, the idea of reservations for her ancestors, the specter of racism, the fact that her mother was raised in an orphanage, that her paternal grandfather had married a schizophrenic, and other adult issues. He dreaded those conversations.

But these revelations were far from that very October, that fair day when Sunny would sit with Hank and Susan and watch Rachel Endless Rain fly around the track with a few other Native girls that finally, in the 1990s, could compete with the boys. Hank knew the significance of that would be lost on Sunny, but it would be a good day of baby animals, whirling rides, caramel corn, and clowns. Hank relaxed.

◀◀◀◆▶▶▶

Opening day at the fair was warm for a fall that had seen red sunsets and early snow. The smells and sounds of livestock, the sight of families admiring crafts and vegetables were comforting and familiar. Neighbors greeted neighbors, placing bets on upcoming races and watching out for each other's kids on the mechanical rides. Four-year-old Sunny was jumping up and down, reluctant to hold her parents' hands, eager to see everything closer, touch everything possible. But Hank and Susan hung on.

The crowds were growing, with many strange faces among the ones they knew. Jason had gone off with Rachel's family to help her get ready for the race. There would be a race for Native American girls separate from the boys, and then another race between the three top riders of each race. They could change horses or not as they wished. Rachel had her own black stallion and a chestnut mare of her father's that Dancing Horse had won on last year. Excitement was building for that event.

The Roses wandered around the flower gardens and crafts tables. Hank dragged them toward a lot full of new tractors and ranch equipment. When they got hungry, Sunny announced, "I don't want caramel corn or any of that stuff. I want Mexican!" They passed up the Indian frybread to find a stand selling homemade tacos and spicy beans. An oddly-dressed man with a bright red bandana around his neck passed by on stilts, and loose dogs hung around begging for food scraps.

The day wore on. Sunny became restless and tired. She shied away from the Ferris wheel and the auction floor. She was such a young and sheltered child. Susan and Hank tried to distract her by going into the cooler indoor barns where lambs and calves were housed. Hank ran into an acquaintance of Julian's, a silver-haired gentleman guarding his grandson's lamb pen. Hank let go of Sunny's hand for a moment to greet the old man. Susan had both arms around her cousin, a younger relation who had found her through old orphanage records, who now lived on the reservation and whom she had not seen for months. The woman cried, "Oh, Susan, how I've missed you! Where's that child? How she must have grown!"

Susan turned toward Hank and said, "She's right here. Sunny? Henry, where's Sunny?" There was some panic in her voice.

"I thought you had her hand," he said, looking around now, imagining their daughter with her body pressed up against a young animal.

"She can't have gone far," Susan said.

"Sunny!" he cried.

Hank turned quickly in all directions, alarm bells going off in his head. He followed the antics of groups of children with an intensity rising with every passing minute. "Susan! You and your cousin go look in that restroom!" He grabbed a security officer that happened to come into the building, almost knocking him down. He couldn't think. He called out Sunny's name again, a wild cry of desperation.

"Sunny! Answer Daddy!"

Susan was running toward the booth where they had eaten the Mexican food. The man on the stilts bent down toward her and shook his head.

Several fair-goers turned toward them and then noticed their distress. People began to search among the pens, asking others if they'd seen the raven-haired, almond-eyed daughter of the Roses, but folks just shook their heads.

Sunny was gone.

◄◄◄◆►►►

The tall lady was walking much too fast for Sunny's little legs. They were twisting and turning through the crowd.

"Where're we going?" Sunny asked.

"To see the puppy, remember? Your daddy wanted me to show you the puppy. Come on," the woman said, jerking her along.

Sunny felt like crying, but she never cried. It had been trained out of her, intentionally or not. She tried to walk faster. Maybe there was really a puppy. She loved puppies. There was a car parked by the exit, a white van with darkened windows. She heard yelping inside, and when the lady opened the door, a black and brown animal lunged at her eagerly.

"Oh! Puppy!" Sunny cried. "You're so big!"

The lady pushed her in the back with the animal and looped a strange metal bracelet around one of her wrists. She clipped it to the place where the puppy-as-big-as-a-dog was chained. Sunny was scared. But she did not cry. Then they were moving slowly out of the parking lot. There were no windows at all in that part of the van. Sunny could see the back of the lady's head, dark brown curly hair with some red sticking out here and there that didn't look real, but nothing else.

"Lady?" Sunny said softly.

"Mommy. My name is Mommy. Say Mommy."

"I have to pee," Sunny said, squeezing her legs together.

A hand came around and slapped her. "Don't talk like that. That is unacceptable. You'll have to wait," she said sharply.

Sunny felt the warm liquid soaking her cowgirl outfit. The large puppy sniffed at her and whined. She hugged it, and it snuggled willingly against her.

"Don't get too attached," the lady said. "It's my dog. You're just the baby."

"No, I'm not," Sunny argued bravely.

"Yes. That's your name now. Baby."

"I want to go home," Sunny said.

"We're going home," the lady said.

And with those words, Sunny fell asleep on the puppy's soft side.

◄◄◄◆►►►

The Roses sat in the Elko County sheriff's office in absolute terror. Hank told Susan they should hold on to the things everyone said—*Kids wander off all the time. Someone will bring her in. No reports of suspicious persons in town.* A detective—Hank had already forgotten his name—said, "We have a great team out there right now looking for your little girl." But the words were hollow and unbelievable.

It had happened so fast. Why didn't Sunny cry out? Why didn't she stay closer to them? They ached to know the answers, to hear her sweet voice, to see her being carried through the door, but none of those things happened. Hank called the ranch, and everyone that was not at the fair spread out in all directions to look for their child, but it gave them small comfort. If Sunny was abducted, she would be hidden, silenced, maybe … no, not hurt … not … *killed.* They couldn't let themselves think *that.* Susan could barely speak, so Hank answered question after question: *Were they having financial trouble? Marital problems? Had they angered anyone? Threatened anyone? Any dissatisfied clients over the years? A fall from a horse? A dog bite?* It was exhausting and ridiculous.

Hank finally slammed his hand down on the table and said, "We're going back to the fairgrounds once more and then home. Someone might call. Someone might want money." They were informed an FBI agent would accompany them. Already there were Amber Alerts out and posters being made with a picture of Sunny sitting happily on Grey Boy. They would be sent throughout Nevada and a few neighboring states as soon as possible. *She could have gone off with a friend,* the authorities suggested. *She could simply be lost in the crowded fairgrounds.* Hank kept arguing. "She knows our phone number! If she's safe, she'd get someone to call us!"

Jason came into the interview room the detectives had set up at the fairgrounds just as Hank and Susan rushed in for news. Jason had searched the livestock barns, the race grandstand, and the game booths. "I've been everyplace! I'm losing my voice from calling her name. Where could she be?" he said.

The gates closed at midnight, but there would still be people checking restrooms, tack trunks, storage tents, even the handful of cars that remained after hours. Roadblocks were set up a few miles away, but it was probably too late.

Hank helped Susan to the truck. They climbed in with their separate visions of what might have happened. Hank glanced around outside the vehicle. Maybe Sunny had tried to find them out there in the parking lot. He looked at Susan and shook his head. He fumbled with the ignition in the dark and then gasped. There, on the dashboard, facing out toward the empty twilight, was the soft and not-to-be-cuddled-soon toy Grey Boy.

4

◄◄◄◆►►►

*S*unny woke with a start. She was cold and still wet and now a little hungry. It was dark outside, and the puppy was being taken away. *"I'll be back for you in a minute. You'd better be quiet,"* the lady said.

"But are we home yet?" she asked softly.

"We're home, Baby, but the dog can't go in the house. I have to chain him outside."

"I'm cold," Sunny whispered.

"Stop your whining and do as Mommy says!"

"Where's my mother?" Sunny asked, squirming and raising her voice.

"I am your mommy!" the lady insisted.

"No, my real *one!" Sunny said. She jerked on the chain that still held her.*

"I am the only mommy that matters now. You'd better get used to it," the lady answered.

Sunny could not see her very well. There was no light anywhere. She began shivering, and a sound bubbled up in her throat. But she did not cry.

◄◄◄◆►►►

After three weeks, Hank and Susan could hardly bear the loss of their daughter. No one had called asking for money. No one had called thinking they might have seen her. Susan had lost ten pounds, and Hank had to beg her to eat. The FBI informed them of every lead, every possible scenario, until Hank had to ask them to stop. "I only want to hear from you the day you find her," he said.

Hank closed the ranch for the winter, and the fierce storms were a constant fear for him. What if the kidnapper didn't have a warm place? What if they were traveling in a car and got stuck in a drift or ran out of gas? He drove himself crazy with these kinds of questions but finally decided he had to be strong for Susan. He had to be hopeful and comforting.

Jason said again and again, "I should have been with Sunny instead of off helping Rachel. She had her whole family. I should have been with you, my family."

Hank tried to put the old man's mind at ease. "You have driven more miles than any of us looking for signs. You have probably prayed too, which I can't do yet. You gave Sunny so much confidence. When she gets scared, she'll think of you. Please don't take any fault with yourself."

But Jason couldn't even answer. He wept openly while Hank knew that, wherever his little girl was, she would not cry.

They went to church. The priest that had blessed Julian and Serena the night before their wedding was in a Catholic nursing home. The new priest embraced them but could offer them no sacraments. Hank might have agreed to join the Church just for someone to talk to, but Susan would never give up her Iroquois traditions. She told Hank she believed more in the spirit of Grey Boy and even in the spirit of Serena, after whom Sunny was named, before any spirit of the white world. The young clergyman promised to light candles for them and for their lost child.

Sometimes, throughout that first winter, the only sound in the main house was the roaring of the fires in the hearths. Susan and Hank ate in silence and made love in silence. They didn't use protection, but they really didn't want another child. They wanted their bright and lovely Serena Sun.

◀◀◀◆▶▶▶

When spring broke the icy grip of winter, pieces of their hearts melted too. Susan said, "Oh, Sunny loved that purple crocus, because it dared to break through the snow!" "This time last year she was climbing up on Grey Boy," Hank remembered. "This is about the time she asked me to put that photo of Julian and Serena in her room." Susan said. These memories brought a certain peace to their existence. All the truths about their child became real again. They believed in her. Hank imagined lengthening the stirrups for her that summer, teaching her to post the trot, having her outfit made for the fair, carrying the blue ribbon or any color ribbon out of the ring. They celebrated her fifth birthday. The FBI did not call.

◀◀◀◆▶▶▶

In a trailer park in Winnemucca, Mommy was talking to Baby about school.

"I should send you to kindergarten. I don't like having you around all day, and I for sure don't want you to be illiterate."

"What does that mean?" Baby asked.

"I want you to read and write and know *things, but I don't want you to tell anyone where you live."*

"Okay," Baby said.

"You know what will happen if you ever do that."

"You'll hurt Dog."

"That's right."

"Why doesn't Dog have a name?" Baby wanted to know.

"He has a name all right, but it's a secret. I'll tell you some day when you can understand it. Don't ask so many questions. Finish your toast."

"I'm tired of toast," Baby cried and threw it on the floor.

"Well, aren't you full of yourself today. Let's just see how it feels to go without toast for a while."

Baby watched as Mommy stuffed loaves of bread high up in the top cabinet. There wasn't much else to eat, except food in cans, and Baby didn't know how to open them nor would she chance Mommy catching her trying. She went to bed hungry.

Mommy heated some soup the next day and gave Dog a handful of dry food but didn't offer anything to Baby. She lost count of the days. The lady called Mommy let her have water and fruit juice. Dog would come over and lie on the couch with Baby, and once a piece of kibble was stuck on his lip. Baby snatched it and swallowed it whole.

Then one morning the lady said, "Mommy has to go to work for a few days. If I fix you a nice meal, will you be good? Will you stay inside and not talk to anyone?"

"Yes. Can I go to school after that?"

"Don't push me, Baby."

Mommy cooked a real chicken and made dressing with toast crumbs, which was delicious. For dessert, they had applesauce. The lady seemed like a mommy at times like these, so Baby tried to please her, and also for the sake of Dog, she had to be good. And really, she would do almost anything to be able to eat.

Mommy was gone for a long time. She had left cooked things in the refrigerator and plenty of jars of water, but she took Dog with her. She said, "If you're not here when I come back, I'll kill this dog, I swear it."

Baby did not doubt her.

When they returned, Mommy had new dresses and some clothes for Baby, in case she started school in the fall.

"You can't show up in those old rags," she said.

Dog lay down immediately on the worn carpet. He looked thin and tired.

"What's wrong with Dog?" Baby asked.

"Oh, he's been having the time of his life," Mommy said.

Baby didn't know what that meant, so she kept quiet. She was glad Mommy was back, because some of the food was tasting funny, and the noises from the other trailers scared her. One time a man came to the front steps and called a name Baby didn't know. She hid behind the couch and was glad Mommy had showed her how to lock the door.

After that, they got a telephone. Mommy made sure Baby wouldn't touch it by saying, "Remember the time you didn't like the toast?"

Baby was terrified of not having enough to eat, so she readily promised to stay away from the black box with numbers and letters. She knew what those signs meant, but Mommy didn't know she knew. She liked having that secret and wondered what other things she knew that could help her figure out who she was. Something was wrong. Out the window, she could see other children playing in the spaces between the trailers or on the small lawns. What were they talking about so easily, calling each other real names like David and Maggie?

One day Mommy went shopping, and Baby gazed at the telephone. Someplace in her memory was a clue that the zero could be poked and a voice would answer. She locked the door, so she'd have time to change her mind if Mommy came back too soon, and she picked up the receiver. She pressed the zero, and a nice-sounding lady said, "Operator. How may I help you?"

"I think I'm with the wrong mommy," Baby said.

"What? No, wait. Don't hang up. What's your name?"

"Baby."

"How old are you?"

"I think five."

"Where do you live?"

"I don't know."

"Does your mother have a name?"

"Just Mommy."

"Can you read your phone number someplace on the instrument ... the phone?" the O lady asked.

"Maybe a one and a six and a two and ..."

Suddenly the door rattled, and Mommy shouted, "Baby, what the hell. Open this door!"

And Baby hung up.

◄◄◄◆►►►

The FBI called near the end of August.

"Mr. Rose, we're sorry to bother you, but we think this is a lead on your daughter you might want to hear," an official voice said.

"Could you give me your ID number?" Hank asked. He wrote down the number and checked his contact list. It was there.

"Okay, sir, go ahead."

"A telephone operator out of Winnemucca alerted us. She had a disturbing call a few nights ago. When she couldn't trace it, she informed us. Apparently a little girl punched the zero on a phone and said, 'I think I'm with the wrong mommy.'"

"Oh God," Hank said. Susan rushed over from behind the counter where she and Luz were setting out lunch plates.

The FBI man continued. "She said her name was Baby and that she thought she was five years old."

Hank turned to his wife. "Susan, it might be her," and then to the detective, "We taught Sunny to use the zero on the phone, and she was five last July! What are the chances of that being another child?"

"It does seem promising, Mr. Rose. The girl read a one and a six and a two off the phone before she was disconnected. We're running down all the numbers in the Winnemucca area with those digits, but there are thousands, as you can well imagine."

"How long will that take?" Hank asked impatiently.

"Several weeks."

"Weeks! She could be long gone from wherever that phone was! I'm going to Winnemucca myself!" He banged his hand down on the counter, knocking a bowl full of grapes to the floor.

"I wouldn't advise that, Mr. Rose. You may compromise the investigation."

"I can't just sit here and do nothing!" Hank shouted into the receiver.

"I understand, Mr. Rose. Give us a week to see what we can turn up. Believe me, we want to find your daughter. This lead means she's still alive. That's great news."

"Yes, sir, thank you," Hank said and thought of the man's last words as he hung up.

Hank repeated the conversation word for word, seeing the disbelief and then the hope come into Susan's eyes.

"I think it's Sunny," she said. She collapsed in a kitchen chair.

"Maybe she'll call the operator again. Maybe she was interrupted. Oh, who could be so cruel as to take another woman's child!"

Hank thought fleetingly that he might know the answer to that but let it pass into the realm of the impossible.

◀◀◀◆▶▶▶

The kidnapper kept her eyes and ears open. She didn't miss much. So when one of her clients with a German shepherd bitch that had contracted for Dog's services stopped her in Walmart and told her about a strange call she'd gotten from the FBI looking for someone with the digits one, two, and six in his or her phone number, the abductor froze for a moment.

"Remember when we first met, we exchanged numbers and thought it was odd both our numbers ended in one-six-two?" the friend said.

"Yeah," Dog's owner said warily.

"Well, this guy said they were looking for a missing child that might be at a place that had those numbers in their phone. I guess I answered all his questions right, and he didn't suspect me, but it was weird."

"Pretty weird. I wonder what's going on. You didn't tell them about me, did you? You know I'm not licensed to breed this dog."

"Oh, no, I knew you didn't have some little girl! Let them do their own research, but sooner or later, they'll probably call. Just thought you should know."

"Thanks. And about that breeding, can we put it off for a few weeks? I have to go to work for a while."

"Sure. Call me when you're ready," the client said.

◀◀◀◆▶▶▶

Mommy raged into the trailer and ripped the phone out of the wall. Baby sat as still as a stone on the couch beside Dog.

"I know what you did!" Mommy screamed.

"Please don't hurt Dog," Baby cried.

"Oh, I'm not going to hurt that dog! I'm going to hurt you! Time for a bath. I'm going to scrub all that deceit right out of you! Now!"

Baby shuddered. She had been dreading baths for a while now. It was a time of soaps and stinging and rough rags and slippery hands, and Baby wasn't sure where all these things might go, just that she felt helpless to control them as though she were not a real person, a child, but someone's doll baby unable even to say, "No, don't do that!" to the lady called Mommy.

Baby resisted at first when the water got high enough for her to climb in the tub. She slid into a corner and pushed the soap out of Mommy's reach. She told Mommy her tummy hurt, but when the lady found the soap and started making suds on the rag, Baby decided to be so quiet that Mommy would forget she was there. She would pretend to be a doll, so the things Mommy did wouldn't be real. But Mommy was playing a different game, getting all worked up and shaking her.

"Where'd you go, huh? Say something! Feel something! There's more where this comes from," Mommy said hoarsely.

What more, Baby could not imagine. But she wanted to go to school, to breathe air that did not smell like Mommy, and to know her name. It seemed to be a very long bath this time.

"You're hurting me," Baby finally had to say, but Mommy said to get over it, all children had to be cleaned up good from time to time, especially now that, because of Baby, they had to move again. The child stared at the objects Mommy had carefully laid out, normal bath things Baby supposed, towels and soaps shaped like pine trees and a hair brush. The bathwater turned pink, and the tree lost its shape, but Baby waited until she was in bed with the lights out. Then the tears fell down her clean, clean cheeks, and sobs tore at her real doll throat.

But even then, she was planning to be the best girl she could be, so maybe Mommy would tell her who she was.

5

◀◀◀◆▶▶▶

S usan and Hank waited for weeks, then months. Sunny turned six somewhere without them, or maybe not. The FBI found no numbers in Winnemucca that matched the residence of a stolen child. They interviewed a woman that had seemed secretive and defensive. She answered their first questions with only a yes or no, but then she finally admitted that she used to have a friend with a similar phone number. "She had a dog but no children. She moved away some time ago," the woman said. She provided no other clues.

When they told the Roses this, sitting in the ranch living room with their notepads and their grave faces, Hank jumped up from the couch. "Dog?" he said. "What kind of dog?"

"A German shepherd, I think," one of the investigators said.

"Henry, what's going on?" Susan asked.

Hank couldn't sit down. He stared at the two detectives, his face pale. "Someone stole a German shepherd from me when I was a kid, that's all. It still bothers me … but it probably has nothing to do with the kidnapping," he said.

"Well, I guess we can't track down everyone with a German shepherd," one of the FBI agents said.

"No … I guess not," Hank admitted. But the coincidence ate at him for days. The stolen puppy would be long dead by now.

Any hope the Roses might have had turned to despair. They tried not to think of where she could be, what she was feeling. Did she remember them, cry for them? No, not cry. Sunny would not cry. But if she was alive, as she got older, she would try to get away, they were certain. When they told this to one of the investigators, a sensitive woman who was still working on finding Sunny long after her assigned time, she shook her head and said, "That's not likely. Many times the kidnapped person is brainwashed into a needy relationship with the abductor. They don't try to escape, especially girls."

Hank sent new posters with an older likeness of his daughter into California and Arizona, even Canada and Mexico. There were crackpots who called wanting ransom, but they could never put Sunny on the line. The Roses were asked to identify bodies of six- and seven-year-olds that were never their child. They held each other and prayed, such as they knew how. They rode into the unforgiving desert, rounded up cattle, planted a garden, and Hank asked once, "Don't you wonder if Sunny will ever see these Nevada sunsets?" as he and Susan faced the multicolored western sky from their swing on the porch. They talked about the times Julian and Serena had sat there watching the same sun in its glorious departure from the darkening azure sky with their own sorrows and fears. But never would Hank's parents know this, this utter helplessness and guilt. Susan and Hank had both let go of Sunny's hand at the moment a monster appeared in her shadow and snatched her from her innocent and beautiful life.

◄◄◄◆►►►

Mommy was happier on the road and too tired at night to hurt her in the bath. Sometimes she let Baby sit in the front seat but always cuffed her to the door. Dog rode in the back of the van and never barked. People didn't notice them.

One day, after they had been driving on Interstate 5 in California, Mommy asked her if she could read that sign, if she knew where they were, and Baby said, "I think it's an I and a five, but what's the N for?"

"I'll tell you later," Mommy said. She pulled into a rest stop that had a small food stand. Baby looked out at all the travelers walking their

dogs in the open, children rolling on the grass and throwing balls to each other. She wondered what that would be like. Then her eyes fell on a tree with a big sign. There was a picture of a girl, just a sketch of what she might look like at age seven. Baby could read the number that had a question mark after it, but she couldn't read all the words. They were too far away, and she had never been to school. One word was a little larger, and she did recognize it, but she didn't know why—NEVADA. She would ask Mommy, because she needed to know why the little girl looked like her.

They had been driving for a long time when Baby thought it safe to ask, "Mommy, what does r-e-w-a-r-d mean?"

Mommy jerked her head around, "Why? When did you see that word?"

"Oh, a long time ago … yesterday," she lied.

"Where?" Mommy insisted.

"On a post someplace. There was a picture of a girl that looked like me. Am I famous?"

"Oh God." Mommy groaned.

She stopped the van and chained Baby in the back with Dog. She slowed down and turned off the highway. They didn't stop to eat all day. Once, Mommy let her and Dog out to pee in the bushes on a lonely stretch of road near dusk. Baby never saw another sign that said REWARD. Mommy never told her what it meant.

The year Baby was seven, she and Mommy lived in Oregon in another trailer park on the outskirts of Ashland. The town was full of artists and actors and visitors from all over the world. There were lots of dogs for Dog to play with—or do whatever Mommy did with him—and people of all shapes and sizes and colors. Sometimes men held hands with men, and there was a black lady in the next trailer with three white-looking children. Nobody paid any attention to a striking red-haired woman and an Indian-looking child.

Baby made no friends and went to bed hungry and sometimes exhausted from Mommy's bath time games. It was better to play than to struggle, and Baby thought maybe all children had to do these things in order to grow up.

"This is easier than I thought it would be," Mommy said once, coming into the trailer with Dog after a long day doing business.

She showed Baby, handcuffed and thirsty beyond belief, a fistful of bills. Some had the number one hundred printed on them.

"Are we going to move now?" Baby asked.

"Why ever do you think that?"

"If we have more money, we could get a house and have more food and maybe have different bedrooms," Baby said hopefully.

"Well, the food and a nice hotel now and then I could do, but we are never going to have separate bedrooms. I'll be old and gray before that happens," Mommy said, not yet releasing the cuffs.

Baby said, "Can I have some water?"

"Sure," Mommy said. "Can I have some of this?" And she started taking Baby's clothes off in the middle of the day.

The weeks passed. When Mommy went out to shop or see dog-people, sometimes without Dog, Baby curled up next to the never-a-puppy gentle animal and tried to sleep. She was afraid to sleep at night because of the things Mommy did that woke her up. She dreamed of the girl on the poster. She lived in a trailer park like Mommy's, didn't have any friends, and cried a lot. But that is one thing Baby would not let herself do—cry.

◀◀◀◆▶▶▶

Baby lost track of the years, but sometime after her eighth birthday, Mommy bought her a few books and tried to teach her how to read. "You might as well not be ignorant all your life," she said.

Baby was grateful and tried to hug her, but Mommy pushed her away. "You don't need to like me, Baby. That's not part of my plan."

Baby had just learned that word plan, so she asked, "Where are we going? Why are we driving so far?"

"Don't make me sorry I gave you those books!"

They left Oregon and slept at run-down motels. Mommy found people to pay her for Dog to visit their dogs. He began to age a little and had no enthusiasm for life. He didn't gobble up his food like he used to *and seemed to want to hide when strangers came too close. Sometimes Baby thought she saw tears in his eyes, so she told him, "Don't worry, Dog. I'll make a plan for us to leave Mommy. We can run in those green fields out there and maybe go back to Nevada. I remember Nevada. Open space and cactus and snow at Christmas, not so many cars or brown skies. You'll like it, Dog, you'll see."*

"What're you mumbling about back there?" Mommy asked.

"Just telling Dog a story," she answered.

"I might as well tell you his name. I think you're old enough to learn it."

But it was a name Baby had never heard. Mommy spelled it out, but Baby could never find it in the dictionary. She asked Mommy what it meant, but she didn't know. It was just a name she liked.

"Is it a place in Nevada?" Baby asked.

"God, child, you're getting too big for your britches!" And she stopped and threw all the books out of the car. For the first time in her entire life, Baby cried out loud. Those books were the key to the world, the key to the cuffs that more and more frequently bound her to Dog, a motel bed, a bar in the back of the van, a tree in an isolated campground.

Baby thought if she read enough, she would discover who she was and make sense of everything else. Mommy fed her and kept her clean, especially those parts Baby hated her to touch, and let her be friends with Dog. Mommy was all she knew. She began to be afraid of all the people outside the van or the motel room. She hid. She didn't talk to anyone. Mommy seemed to like her as a shy Baby and encouraged her to be a silent, good girl so she and Dog could go off and make money to keep them alive.

◀◀◀◆▶▶▶

The summer she was nine, Baby tried to count the marks she had scratched in the van in the dingy white paint. There were eight marks, but she wasn't sure how old she was when she began to keep track of the years. She would glance at calendars in gas stations and motel laundry rooms, and when a month she had chosen as the one *came around again, she took a tool from Mommy's car-bag and dug into the inside of the back door. One thing she was sure of—she was older than the girl on the poster.*

They turned off the road called 5 and took one called Highway 101. It was a warm and, what Baby called, a friendly season. She saw the ocean for the first time and couldn't believe her eyes. "Oh, oh," she cried. A vast expanse of roiling water and waves that went on forever, a color she had no name for. "What's that called? Why is it so noisy? Can I touch it?"

She asked ten questions all at once, and Mommy jerked her arm viciously. "I can't drive while you're jabbering," she said.

Baby said, "Mommy, why are you keeping me when I'm so much trouble?"

"I am exacting revenge."

Baby had no idea what that meant and was afraid to know. She just asked, "Can I go to school now?"

"Maybe in the fall," Mommy answered cautiously. "I could certainly make more money with you in school. What would we call you?"

"My name is Baby."

"But we can't use that. Kids would tease you. It's not a good school name."

"Sunny," Baby said suddenly.

Mommy punched her arm hard. "Why on earth did you say that?"

"I don't know. It just sounded right."

"Well, it's not right. It's a silly name. You'll be Patricia."

"I hate that. Why can't I have an Indian name?"

"Do you think you're Indian?"

"Maybe. In a book, there were pictures of Indian children. I kind of look like that," Baby suggested.

"How 'bout Rainbow?" Mommy gave in.

"Okay."

"But you're still Baby to me," she insisted.

"Okay," Baby said, thinking of the first day of school. As scared as she would be of the people, there would be books and maybe paints. She had dreamed of holding brushes and dabbing them in the colors of the world

*she had seen, the new places. She'd paint the Pacific Ocean—Mommy
had told her its name—the redwood trees, the miles of vineyards and
meadows full of horses and cows. She had wanted to stop once when
they first saw the horses. There was a small, grey-colored one right by
the fence, but Mommy had said no, they were evil creatures.*

*Baby looked back for a long time at the white fence and the grey face
reaching over the top for fresher grass, and her heart pounded fiercely
in her chest. She wanted to stop to see if it was real. She wanted to pull
up the wild oats that were just out of the animal's reach and feed him
out of her hands. She thought of different names that would fit him as
he disappeared from sight. She knew that horse.*

‹‹‹◆›››

Grey Boy sat on a windowsill in Sunny's bedroom in Nevada, the last
rays of a bitter summer sun raining bleakly on his lonely gaze.

‹‹‹◆›››

The Roses were forty now. They were not going to have any more
children. Uncle Jason died that year, Hank and Susan were sure, of a
broken heart. It seemed he had come into their lives for Sunny and
could not stay without her. He, too, was buried at the canyon house
where he was born but at some distance from Julian and Serena,
respecting the break in his relationship with his brother, the hurt
feelings buried in the same ground.

Hank had sold most of the cattle and the horses. He kept the
best riding mounts for his family and loyal wranglers and the few
friends who came out to ride with them. They tried to join a support
group for parents who had suffered the loss of a child to abduction,
missing still or entrenched in some odd landscape, but they just
couldn't hear those stories over and over or look at the grim, tear-
stained faces or hug another grieving mother or father. *Do we appear
to others like that? Gaunt and round-shouldered and utterly hopeless?*
Hank wondered.

Hank taught Susan to ski, and they pushed out across the country that winter into the forbidding white desert, stopping to breathe heavily and wondering if Sunny was feeling as alone as they were. They talked about the kidnapper. Was it a man who might be abusing her? A woman who couldn't have a child and took theirs for her own? Was someone still hoping for a ransom but didn't know how to contact them? Could someone have killed her when she began to struggle or ask too many questions? Which she surely would. It was her nature. They skied on a few miles, letting the pain in their hearts transfer to their legs and lungs, pressing their feet into the cold tracks as if branding the kidnapper with pent-up rage.

Then spring came and the hot, dusty summer of Sunny's ninth birthday, the only storms in the psyches of Hank and Susan. They grew close, which was a blessing. Some marriages they knew didn't hold together after the gut-wrenching loss of a child. They watched their friends' children grow and change, show their animals, act in the school plays, and march in the band on parade days. To them, Sunny was still the petite four-year-old sitting on Jason's shoulders, the curious youngster helping her dad turn the pages of Walter Farley's *The Black Stallion* that Hank read to her every night, the serious little equestrian scrambling up on Grey Boy with her child's enthusiasm. But that girl would never return. That girl had truly died, even if she were still breathing, someplace.

No one went to the fair that October, but the ranch honored Sunny's disappearance with a small ceremony. Everyone gathered in the round pen with Grey Boy, now fifteen, and showered him with carrots and apples. Native Americans, Latinos, and two African friends of Akmal's danced around the missing child's horse, and prayers were sent to heaven in three or four languages.

6

◀◀◀◆▶▶▶

That fall, Mommy enrolled Baby in a private school near Solvang, California. She had traded the van, which really smelled like Dog and other things, for a nice car and dyed Baby's hair to hide the black tresses. It came out kind of orange, so Mommy cut it short and put some makeup on her face to lighten her skin. She was small for her age, probably from not eating right, so Mommy wanted to put her in the third grade and hoped her lack of education wouldn't show too much there.

The principal was a soft-spoken, fiftysomething woman. Mommy told her they had been traveling and didn't have any records with them.

"Your name is Rainbow?" the woman asked Baby.

"Yes, ma'am," Baby said, not meeting her eyes.

"You may call me Mrs. Whittlesey."

"Okay."

"How long has it been since you were in school?" the principal asked.

Baby glanced at Mommy, who was now called Ellen Page and had blonde hair instead of her flaming red.

"A couple of years," Mommy Page said. "I bought her some books."

"Can you read, Rainbow?" Mrs. Whittlesey asked.

"A little," Baby answered.

The principal handed her a third grade reader and pointed to a paragraph. Baby could read it easily but didn't know what all the words meant.

"*How old are you?*"

Again the look at Mommy.

"*She's just eight,*" *Mommy lied.*

"*Do you have a permanent address, Mrs. Page?*"

"*It's* Miss, *and no, we're not settled yet. I'll let you know.*"

"*Well, Rainbow, would you like to start tomorrow?*"

At first Baby didn't respond. She wasn't used to being called Rainbow. Mommy nudged her.

"*Oh yes, that would be good,*" *Baby said with true fervor.*

"*Okay, then. I'll introduce you to the class. Your teacher is Mr. Bowen. You'll like him. He's great with new kids.*"

"*We'll be back in the morning,*" *Mommy promised. "Is that all right?*"

"*Yes … school starts at 8:20. I'll meet you here in the office,*" *Mrs. Whittlesey said. She ushered them out.*

Baby was beyond excited. There were so many books in the principal's office. Maybe Mr. Bowen would know where Nevada was, maybe even the meaning of Dog's name. There were so many things she wanted to know, but she had to be careful. Mommy didn't like her asking too many questions.

They went to a motel. Mommy had bought some hamburgers in a drive-through restaurant on the way there. They watched some television, something Mommy rarely allowed. Dog moved around restlessly in the stuffy room. Then Mommy said, "We'd better get you cleaned up for school."

Baby flinched.

"*Oh, I'm not going to hurt you! Come on.*"

For the first time, Baby felt she had a choice. She could run. Maybe find that nice Mrs. Whittlesey. Or she could submit to Mommy and go to school. She chose school and dragged herself into the bathroom. There was no bathtub, just a shower.

"*Well, come on, off with those clothes. You can wear one of the new dresses tomorrow.*"

Baby slowly undressed. Mommy watched with interest but seemingly without her usual intentions. She simply helped Baby soap her grimy flesh from their days on the road in the hot car. Then she slipped off her own clothes and lifted the girl up by her firm buttocks so that Baby's legs wrapped around her. The frightening but suddenly gentle woman swung Baby in slow circles under the warm spray on the cool tile. Her hands were everywhere, but there was no pain, only the pain in the center of Baby's being that screamed at Mommy to stop. She thought of school and relinquished herself to the unwanted and unholy dance.

◄◄◄◆►►►

The school bell rang. Mrs. Whittlesey led her by the hand into Mr. Bowen's classroom. No girl had on a dress. The boys laughed at her. The teacher shushed them. "We have all been new someplace in our lives. Let's behave like gentlemen and ladies." Baby liked him immediately.

Mrs. Whittlesey said, "Class, this is Rainbow, and she hasn't been to school for a while. Who is willing to help her?"

Several girls raised their hands and a couple of boys. Baby didn't know what to think of them. She had never spoken to another child. How would she know the right things to say? She began to feel a little sick.

The principal left her with a room full of strangers. Mr. Bowen asked if she could read the blackboard from the fifth row where there was a seat.

"Yes," answered Baby, and the teacher handed her a blank notebook, a pencil, and a couple of books. She looked at those with awe. It felt like the first day of her life. She would do anything to keep that feeling.

Mr. Bowen was rapping a stick on his desk. "Open your geography books to page sixty-three."

Baby turned the pages lovingly and then almost cried out when she read the word: Nevada. *Mommy had never told her about God, but she had read what she could in the Bibles in motel rooms, and it seemed the hand of God was over her in that moment as she looked at that word.*

She couldn't read all the words but listened intently when the other children read sections aloud. Mr. Bowen didn't call on her that day, and she was grateful. She saw on a map how close she was to Nevada, just the next state away. She heard about gambling and taxes, which bored her, and then about deserts and mountains and cattle ranches and wild horses, which touched her very soul. Why would Mommy have taken her from such a wonderful place? Was she the girl on the poster?

"Okay," Mr. Bowen was saying, "your homework is to find out something about Nevada that we didn't read today. You may use newspapers, television, the Internet, friends, or relatives."

None of these were very available or reliable for Baby. Not even her own mommy would talk about Nevada. But she already knew what she would say and couldn't wait for her turn in class.

At home that night, Mommy quizzed her about school. "What are you studying?"

"The states of America."

"Which state?"

"California," Baby lied.

"Oh, okay. Anything else?"

"How to measure things with a ruler and make figures like triangles and squares."

"Did you make any friends?" Mommy wanted to know.

"No," Baby said truthfully, and Mommy relaxed.

◀◀◀◆▶▶▶

Mr. Bowen didn't call on her right away. She was nervous but sure of her facts, well, fairly sure. Some of it, perhaps, she made up, but no one could check it.

"Rainbow, have you had time to do your homework?"

"Yes, Mr. Bowen, I'm ready," she said.

"Okay, then."

And Baby began to speak. "Out on the highway for many days and many miles, my mommy and I saw big signs posted on trees and buildings and telephone poles. The first word that we noticed was Nevada in large, black letters. Then there was a picture of a girl as she might look at seven or eight years old, then another word—Reward. Mommy told me a little girl had been kidnapped in Nevada, and her parents were so sad and giving a reward to whoever found her, dead or alive. Mommy said the whole state of Nevada was searching for this child and maybe we could find her and *get the money. People in Nevada have lots of money and horses and love their children very much. That's my story that wasn't in the book."*

There was an eerie silence in the room. No one moved. Mr. Bowen finally said, "That was amazing, Rainbow. You noticed a real life, a palpable—put that word on your vocabulary list—fact, not just heights of mountains or the winners of 4-H events at fairs." Then he wrote the word palpable *on the board in tall letters and told them to copy it into their notebooks. "It's a big word, but if Rainbow can tell that story, if you can hear that story and feel its truth, you are ready for that word."*

Baby was proud, but something lingered at the back of her mind, something Mr. Bowen had said. After class, she approached the teacher cautiously. She was drawn to his open face, his gentle eyes. She trusted him, but she whispered haltingly, "I know something else about Nevada, Mr. Bowen."

"You do?"

"Yes … that little girl was kidnapped at a fair."

"How do you know? Was that on the poster?"

"No. I just know. I think it's a secret, but I wanted to tell you."

"I'm glad you did, Rainbow. You can tell your mother you got an A today."

◀◀◆▶▶

That afternoon, when Rainbow got home from school, Mommy was pacing the floor in the motel room. "Something's wrong with Dog." She used Dog's real name, but Baby didn't understand it yet. She'd have to ask Mr. Bowen if he knew what it meant. "I have to find a vet. I'll have to leave you alone. Can I trust you?"

"Yes, Mommy," Rainbow said as earnestly as she could. The world was just beginning to make sense. She wasn't going to ruin it now.

Mommy donned the blonde wig. She had thrown out the brown one a long time ago. She dragged Dog to the car. Baby turned on the TV and switched channels until she found a movie about a black horse and a girl about her age. Suddenly, she remembered the feeling of a horse between her legs. She remembered how to go up and down with the horse's trot.

She remembered an old man lifting her into the saddle. She remembered an Indian man looking between the rails of a corral and saying, "That's good, Sunny." Sunny? Who's Sunny? Mommy will say I dreamed it, she thought and set her mind to figuring out how to tell Mommy about the A in geography. But she knew it was too risky.

◄◄◄◆►►►

Dog got vitamins, and Mommy never heard about the A. Mommy heard less and less of what Baby Rainbow was thinking or doing. The girl talked to her about math and art, about the few friends she made, but nothing to scare Mommy or challenge her. Things went smoothly for a while. One day near the end of the first semester, she asked Mr. Bowen about Dog's name.

"Oh, yes, that's a Spanish word. You'll learn that with Mrs. Ybarra next year."

"But can't you tell me what it means?" Rainbow asked.

"I think you're a smart enough girl to discover that for yourself. I will say, I think that's a strange name for a dog."

◄◄◄◆►►►

In the spring before Baby's tenth birthday, the posters were removed from all the places they had been nailed and read and weathered and forgotten. Mr. Bowen drove up 101 on his Easter vacation, eager to prove Rainbow's story, but he could find no evidence of a missing girl from Nevada. The presence of Rainbow and her strong convictions about the matter haunted him, however, and he would not disbelieve her outright. He would pay attention to any clues about her past that might shed light on this amazing child. She was reading at the sixth grade level now and seemed to have information, for example, about horses, that her current lifestyle could not have provided.

He remembered a day in class when some child said baby horses were called colts. Rainbow piped right up, "No, that's not right. Boy babies are colts, and girl babies are fillies." Then, on another day, two students were arguing about whether or not horses could dance. Rainbow quietly informed them, "Yes, they can dance. It's called dressage."

Bowen had asked, "Rainbow, how on earth do you know what *that* means?"

"I've seen an Indian practicing some moves. He told me it was dressage."

"But when? Where in your life?" he persisted.

"I don't know," she said. "Somewhere on a big desert. And there was music playing. I'd know it if I heard it again."

The chance of him finding that music was so slim that he didn't pursue it.

She asked him once, "Could you call me Nevada instead of Rainbow?"

"I don't think your mother would like that," he'd answered.

"No, probably not. She hates Nevada."

"Why is that?"

"I think she got hurt there, and that's why she doesn't want to lose me."

"Why would she lose you, sweetheart?"

"I'm not sure. In some pictures in my head I have of my life, she's not in them," the girl said.

"Memory can play tricks on you," he said.

"I know a trick," she said, brightening a little.

"You do?"

"Yes. How to get out of handcuffs!"

Mr. Bowen thought of that later with chills. Handcuffs? He checked her wrists for marks after that as he gave her books or paintbrushes. There were never any signs that she had been bound. But soon, she would be out of his care, so he didn't dwell on her unusual pronouncements.

◄◄◄◆►►►

During that same spring break, Mommy moved to a different motel. Dog regained some energy, and Baby was usually lost in a book. Mommy questioned her about everything. Mostly Baby lied. Mommy didn't even know the word palpable. *Baby could lead her off on any direction without revealing her coveted education.*

But one thing she could not do was keep Mommy's hands off of her. The woman was careful not to leave marks on the outside that someone could see. But there were marks on the inside, and one day, Mr. Bowen asked her to stay after school. Baby shifted from one foot to the other, anxious to get to where Mommy was waiting for her.

"Rainbow, you have been so quiet lately. Is everything okay?"

"Yes." Baby paused. "I think I need more to eat." Baby was scrambling for some viable—new vocabulary word—reason to explain her withdrawal from class activities. She would never *tell what Mommy did to her night after night. But things got scary, because just then, Mommy raced into the school when Baby didn't come right to the car. She confronted Mr. Bowen.*

"What's going on here?" Mommy demanded.

"Why, nothing, Miss Page."

Mommy's wig had slipped, and a piece of bright red hair showed on one side of the kidnapper's pretty face. Would Mr. Bowen notice?

He only said, "Sorry to worry you. I was just asking Rainbow if she should be eating healthier food. She's been tired and losing a little weight."

"She's just having a growth spurt. I'll get her more vegetables and maybe some protein powder, okay? Now, let's go, Rainbow."

Rainbow went with Mommy down the hall. There was Mrs. Whittlesey just coming out of her office.

"Rainbow, how nice to see you! I hear you're doing well in third grade and may skip to fifth next year."

"I guess so," Rainbow admitted. She had not told Mommy of this possibility, although Mr. Bowen had mentioned it several times lately.

"She's way too young for that class," Mommy said. "I'll put her in fourth grade if it's all the same to you."

"Well, of course, it's your decision. Rainbow is a smart girl. I'm sure she'll find her place in this world, in spite of us," the principal said agreeably.

But Mommy mumbled all the way out to the car and finally said, "Have you been talking to these teachers?"

"Only about school stuff," Baby answered, and that was true. What else could she really talk about? She didn't even know her real name. It was not Rainbow, and it was not Baby. But here she was in California, growing up, learning history and math and creative writing. She loved school and couldn't give it up for a world she didn't know.

"Mommy," she said on the way home, "thank you for letting me go to school. You are the best mommy. I'll never leave you."

Mommy reached over and grabbed her hand. "You sweet-talkin' me?"

"No, Mommy. I really, really mean it."

The kidnapper squeezed her hand. "Thanks, kid."

◄◄◄◆►►►

That summer, they took a trip to Santa Barbara. Mommy loved the ocean and shops and the number of people who had dogs like hers who might want Dog's puppies and pay big bucks—*Mommy's words. They walked on the beach late in the day when all the vacationers and families who lived there were gone. Dog got to run a little, but Mommy held fast to Baby's hand.*

"Can I go into the water?" Baby asked.

She thought she would just keep going into the forbidding but safer-than-the-bathtub frothy water. Mommy surely would not follow her in there.

"Do you think I'm crazy? You don't know how to swim, Baby. What gave you the idea you could just walk into the ocean?"

"It looks cool."

"Are you hot? Are you coming down with something?" Mommy asked, putting her hand on Baby's forehead.

"I don't think so. I'm just curious about it, that's all."

"Well, think about this: this is a nice town," Mommy said.

Baby didn't want to move but could see it coming.

"There'll be good teachers here, too."

"I hope so," Baby said, resigned to the idea of starting over in a new place.

But they didn't make it back to Santa Barbara before school started, so Baby Rainbow entered Mrs. Ybarra's fourth grade class stronger and more determined than ever to study the world and see what it could do for her. Most of the kids had come from Mr. Bowen's class, and she recognized a few of the girls who had befriended her.

The first thing the young Hispanic teacher gave them was a Spanish/English dictionary. Rainbow looked up Dog's name as fast as she could. She was unsure of the spelling, but suddenly, there it was before her eyes: Paraíso—paradise. She raised her hand and asked Mrs. Ybarra how to pronounce it.

"Why do you want to know that word?"

"It's the name of my ... my mommy's dog," she answered bravely. (Mommy would kill her.)

"It must be a very good dog," the teacher said.

"He brings us money," Rainbow admitted.

Mrs. Ybarra gave her a funny look.

Baby loved Spanish and was soon far ahead of her classmates in that subject and everything else. But Mrs. Ybarra asked her why her last name—Page—wasn't Mexican. That made Baby very uneasy, and she didn't answer.

"Rainbow Page? That's not a Mexican name," the teacher said.

"I'm not Mexican, Mrs. Ybarra."

"Well, what are you?"

Baby thought of the first thing that maybe made sense. She thought of the brown-skinned man on the dressage horse on the desert and said, "I'm an Indian."

Just then, Mr. Bowen came in. The Spanish teacher told everyone to copy some vocabulary lists from the blackboard and stepped into a back corner of the classroom with him. They spoke in Spanish, and Baby understood every word they said.

"Why is that girl's name not Latino?"

"She's not Mexican, Lola. Haven't you met the mother?"

"No."

"Hm. Lucky you."

"What about the father?" Mrs. Ybarra ventured.

"Don't know, but I don't think Mexican. I do think that we may have a child at risk here, however, so keep an eye on her."

"Of course, Allen. I can see how sensitive she is about certain subjects. I must say she's obsessed with Nevada."

"I know. Just be careful with her."

"I will."

◀◀◆▶▶

Everyone was careful with Baby. No one wanted to be confronted by Ellen Page. But Mrs. Whittlesey called Rainbow into the office and asked her if she wanted to skip fifth grade next year, and Baby smiled with hope.

"You shouldn't be kept in a class that you have surpassed," the nice principal told her. "I remember that day when I visited Mrs. Ybarra's room and you recited that story about a country named Paradise, all in Spanish. That was exceptional."

But one day near the end of the school year, Mommy appeared and informed everyone that she and her daughter were moving. Mrs. Whittlesey came and took Rainbow out of class, and Baby stood awkwardly in the hallway while the now almost-red-haired-again Ellen Page explained she'd found a cousin farther south that wanted them to live with her.

"Farther south where?" the principal asked.

"I don't think you need to know that," Mommy said.

"Well, to send the school records and—"

"When we get settled, I'll have the new school request them," Ellen promised. She had her arms folded, one foot tap, tap, tapping on the hardwood floor.

"Mrs. Whittlesey, I'll be all right. Please don't worry about me," Rainbow said because the principal had a doubtful look on her face. The woman handed Rainbow a business card with her personal phone number on it. Baby tried to put it in her pocket, but Mommy got it out of her hands and later destroyed it.

Baby felt empty. She felt like crying and couldn't remember why she *didn't cry as a young child. She had outgrown all her clothes. Her hair was brittle and dull from all the dyeing. How could she ever be herself when she would always be what Mommy wanted her to be?*

On the way to Santa Barbara, Dog laid his head in Baby's lap in the backseat. He sighed. Baby knew his apathy—the last word on her vocabulary list. Her solace was books. Who knew where those would come from now? For Dog, the good dog Paraíso, there was only food and female dogs. No play, no open fields, no sensible name, no love.

7

◄◄◄◆►►►

Hank and Susan opened the ranch for a short season the summer Sunny would be ten, wherever she was. They still had Tyrone and Dancing Horse, Billy and Angie, who were loyal and experienced wranglers. A few new, younger hands filled out the crew. Susan busied herself in the garden with Luz, and Hank made calls to former clients whose children were now of an age to enjoy the riding and branding and hikes in the flowered hills. A feeling of purpose had blossomed with the rosy prickly pear, the silver cholla, and the rare rein-bog orchids that lined creeks and springs. Hank bought a half-dozen well-broke horses. The round pen was cleared of weeds, and Dancing Horse taught everyone the moves he had learned from Serena.

The Native American climbed into the sixty-foot-diameter ring with someone who was afraid of horses, and maybe the horse was a little afraid too. He gave a rope or a buggy whip with surveyor tape tied at the end to the client and said, "Now just get the horse moving. Don't scare him. You stay in one place; don't let him run over you." Pretty soon, the horse usually bent his face inward so that his eye showed. "Drop the whip! Drop it!" Dancing horse whispered. Then, if the horse actually turned and stepped toward the person, he said, "Okay, step back now. Let him find you. If he gets close enough to touch, stroke him, praise him, don't catch him up yet. You have a long ways to go." But the client sometimes choked up that such a simple thing could be the beginning of understanding between the horse and the human.

The Roses found themselves laughing and singing around the campfire. The trails enfolded them, felt safe and familiar. They could even listen to stories about Julian and Serena and about Hank when he was the age of their missing daughter. Billy said once, "I remember when little Hank, must've been about four, followed Julian and his guest riders out of sight of the ranch house on his first pony. Ol' Sparkle went about a mile and planted his feet. Serena came along and rescued him, taking him out to his dad on her horse. By then, Hank was so tired and cranky he told everyone his mother *made* him gallop all the way out there! Julian took him back on his horse because he said he had a story to tell Hank as a lesson. I don't know what his dad told him, but Hank never tried that again!"

"I know what he told me," Hank said. "About the time he got bit by the rattlesnake, and if he'd been alone, he probably would have died. That stuck with me for a long time."

"I remember," Angie said. "I rode back for the truck, and then Serena and I drove him to the hospital. Serena held him all the way there and back. She couldn't hide her affection for him. I'd call it love, but they had only met the day before! It was just eerie. Julian was always kind of reserved with people, private, you know, but he let that girl fuss over him … it was something to see."

"I wanted Sunny to know her," Hank said. "I wanted that so bad."

One Saturday night, as fall chased the Roses and their guests inside, Tyrone started playing "Almost Paradise," and Hank had to stop him. "I think I need a different song from now on," he said.

Fewer and fewer clients came as fall brought biting winds and horses started to grow their winter coats, which meant they couldn't be ridden too hard or they wouldn't cool down properly, their sweat turning to cold ice under their thick hair.

Finally, Rancho del Cielo Azul gave up its fall glory to the hand of winter. It was a bitter time for Hank and Susan, a dead season, their child almost dead to them now. They stopped looking at her baby pictures, the ones of her first walking and first sitting in her English saddle on Grey Boy, the few of her with her granduncle Jason, and the last one, taken at the entrance to the fair in September 1997. They stopped going into her room where her games and toys and clothes had not been touched. *Where has the time gone?* Hank thought.

In that frame of mind, the Roses watched winter drift down upon them. They didn't ski until after Christmas, pushing slowly through about a mile of snow and then turning back toward the ranch. They passed some fence that was down and then the gravesite of Julian's grey horse. They halted in their tracks for a moment until tears were freezing on their cheeks.

Warming up by the fire later that night, Hank said to his Iroquois wife, "What do you think about adopting a child, maybe an orphan from Tanzania or from your orphanage La Casa de la Paz in New Mexico?"

Susan nodded slightly but didn't say anything.

"Maybe we're meant to save another child, if we can't save our own."

"It would feel like giving up on Sunny," she said.

"What do you think *she* would want?" Hank asked.

"To trust the Great Spirit," she said.

Right then, Hank didn't trust anything he couldn't see before his very eyes.

◀◀◀◆▶▶▶

Spring came, but for the first time the purple crocus bursting through the snow did not give them hope. Susan stood at the window that faced the long driveway. She was holding the toy Grey Boy. Hank came in from morning chores and put his arms around her.

She said, "You know, Henry, even if Sunny walked up the drive this minute, I wouldn't know what to do. It would not be our little Sunny bouncing around on the real Grey Boy, sitting in Jason's lap for a story, and giving us baby kisses at bedtime. She could almost be anybody's daughter but ours. Look out there at her horse nibbling at the early grass. Would he be too small for *that* girl? Would he recognize her? Would he remember the feel of her hands and legs? No. So how could we know *that* girl?"

"I don't know, darling. We can't think like that. We have to love her still, whether she's dead or alive."

"Oh, it's so hard. It's so hard," Susan said as another chunk of snow slid off the roof and crashed onto the ground below.

◀◀◀◆▶▶▶

There was no snow in the spring in California. Mommy and Baby rarely had to wear sweatshirts, and the grass was green everywhere. Baby had not gone to school that year, so when she saw the school buses, she leaped for joy deep down inside. They had turned off the highway that day to find a hamburger stand. Baby noticed kids walking home from school and the big, yellow buses stopping at certain streets. Mommy got mad because she would have to stop when she got behind them. Finally, she swerved around one and sped off.

Almost at once, some red lights blinked behind their car. Mommy swore and told Baby to keep her mouth shut. She hadn't put the handcuffs on Baby that day and had let her sit in the front seat. Dog was big enough to take up the whole backseat. When Mommy pulled over and turned the engine off, Dog sat up and stared out the window.

"Maybe that'll scare the guy off!" Mommy said.

But it wasn't a guy. It was a girl. She asked Mommy for her driver's license. "You from Nevada?" the police lady asked.

"Yeah," Mommy said.

"Your license expires next month."

"I'll take care of it," Mommy said. "We're just visiting some friends. We'll be back home before then."

"Do you know why I stopped you?" the lady said.

"Not sure."

"You can't pass a school bus when it's letting students off and has the stop arm out and its red signals flashing."

"I didn't see the … stop arm," Mommy said.

"Since you're from out of state, I'll just give you a warning this time, but be careful. This is an important law."

She peered in more closely at Baby.

"This your child?"

"Yes," Mommy said.

"What's your name, honey?" the nice lady said to Baby.

"She's retarded," Mommy jumped in. "That's why she's not on one of those buses."

"She doesn't look like you," the police lady said.

"She looks like her father," Mommy told her.

Baby wondered if the woman would believe her if she said she wasn't Mommy's child, but just then, Dog growled, and the lady stepped back.

"On your way then," she said.

Mommy drove more slowly after that, and Baby asked, "Do I look like my father?"

"Not one bit!" Mommy said. She laughed for a long time and even almost choked on her hamburger when she tried to say "not one bit" again.

Baby tried another question. "Am I retarded?"

"You sure as hell aren't!" she said.

"Are we really going back to Nevada?"

"Now that is surely a stupid question!" Mommy said. "Finish your burger. You can give some to Dog."

In just a few miles, the highway came really close to the Pacific Ocean. People in black suits were out in the cold water riding the waves. Dog barked at them when they ran up on the beach with long, wooden boards. The sand was white and sparkling and reminded her of something. She longed to walk on it, to feel her feet on it, to hold it in her hand. Mommy told her they were far south of Santa Barbara, the town they had visited last year, but here was that sand again.

"How far does the sand go?" Baby asked.

"A long, long ways," Mommy said. "You will never see the end of it, although it's tempting."

"What's … tempting?" Baby meant what did the word mean, but Mommy answered literally.

"*The sand goes clear into another country where no one would ever find us,*" *she said.*

"*So* tempting *means something you want to do but probably won't?*"

"*Sometimes your questions aren't so stupid, Baby,*" *Mommy said.*

She took an off-ramp and turned around right then and headed back to Santa Barbara.

◀◀◀◆▶▶▶

That July, Baby was eleven, although she didn't know it. The van with the marks was long gone, and they had moved so much she quit trying to line up sticks or save buttons in a little pile that never added up right. Mommy told everyone she was nine or ten, wanting to keep her a baby as long as she could, Baby supposed.

They camped out on the beach while the weather was warm. Mommy met a lot of dog people who admired Dog—Baby didn't dare call him Paraíso; Mommy wouldn't want her to be so smart. Lots of these people arranged to have Mommy's dog mate with theirs. Baby had figured out what mating meant from television. Sometimes it was a good thing and sometimes not. If you did it for love, it was okay. But if you made money from it, even to survive, that was wrong. When you did something wrong, you had to go to church and start over. So Baby asked Mommy why they didn't go to church.

"*Only losers go to church,*" *she said.*

"*Well, I don't care so much about church anyway,*" *Baby said, "but I do care about school.*"

"*Oh, I know. I'm looking into it,*" *Mommy said.*

One time, some kids were playing in the sand, making forts and letting the waves topple their creations as the tide rolled in. They all screamed and pushed each other around in the salty foam. Baby felt as if she were a hundred years old. When had she ever played like that? When had she laughed and walked someplace with a friend? Seen a movie, except on television? The mothers were lovingly brushing sand from their children's eyes and opening up chests with sandwiches and milk. She longed for that life.

But the hardest thing she had to face that summer was the sight of people riding horses along the shore, galloping out into the sea and then back to safer ground before the waves crashed against them. One woman on a shiny chestnut trotted up very close to where she and Mommy had made camp. Baby walked out to meet her. Mommy was busy discussing Dog's services with a couple of men. The rider pulled the horse to a stop and said, "Are you all right, little girl?"

"I don't know," Baby said. "I have a memory of being on a horse, but I think it was just a dream. May I touch him?"

"Sure. Come on, get on! He can carry two."

And before Baby could protest, the woman reached her hand down and lifted her onto the horse's back. Mommy turned around at that very moment and yelled, "Get off that horse this instant!" But the woman didn't hear her and kicked the horse into a canter. They were headed right into the ocean. Baby shrieked, but the horse was smooth and confident beneath them. The rider turned him at the last minute, and they galloped parallel to the pounding waves. Then they were in the waves, the horse's hooves striking the deepening water, then striking only water as it rose up to his chest. It felt to Baby as if the woman and the horse and she were one being, a sea-animal surging through an element all its own.

The woman galloped with Baby back toward the spot where Mommy was frantically waving her hands.

"Your mom doesn't like horses?" The woman raised her voice over the sound of the hooves on the sand.

"She thinks the devil is in them," Baby said, barely able to breathe again.

"You don't believe that!"

"No, I've never believed that," Baby said.

They reached the place on the beach where Mommy paced a little, and the nice lady halted the horse. Baby swung her right leg over the haunches of the seawater-slick animal and landed on her feet. Some wave in her body felt like freedom.

"Nice move, young lady! You've done that before! I hope you're not in too much trouble."

"Yeah, me too."

But, of course, she was in all kinds of trouble. Mommy wouldn't punish her right there on the beach, but Baby knew it would come later.

"I think we'd better find a motel, so we can clean you up. You're a mess," Mommy said.

Baby glared at her.

"Then maybe we'll talk about school."

That was the magic word.

"Okay, Mommy."

Later, Mommy seemed to have forgotten about the horse; she was so intent on removing every grain of salt from every pore in Baby's skin, every opening where it could have entered. The child closed her eyes and took herself out of the arms of the kidnapper. She took herself to the mountainous swells of the Pacific Ocean, to the back of the beautiful horse that had danced in the blue-green sea.

◄◄◄◆►►►

She had to go to fifth grade, even though she knew more than most of the children in the class and was a year older than most of them, she was pretty sure. Mommy told the headmaster of the new school she was nine. It seemed that she was going to be nine forever.

Here the classrooms were crowded. There were many children with dark skin, the children of migrant workers, Mommy said, nothing like her.

"What am I?" she asked Mommy.

"I don't know. I truly don't. You have almond-shaped eyes, but you're not Asian. You have bronze skin, but you're not black or Latino."

"If you're my mommy, why don't you know who I am?"

"Oh, I know who you are. I just don't know everything you are. Does that answer your question?"

"Not exactly."

"Well, I'm doing the best I can! You can be a pain in the ass, but I wouldn't give you up for all the tea in China, you with your almond-shaped eyes. Hah!"

This time Mommy had chosen a Catholic school that offered

scholarships to poor children, which Baby certainly was. "Maybe you'll learn to tell the truth and to follow Mommy's rules better," she said.

Baby just said, "Okay," and allowed herself to be handed over to a short man with a wide smile wearing a long brown dress and a gold cross around his neck. He led her to the first class, chatting about the profusion of God's wildflowers on the nearby hills.

"I'm Father Michael," he said.

It seemed like Sunday school, even though Baby had never been to church that she could remember. Every day began with Bible reading and then prayer. The kids that memorized the verses they read got extra points. If you said your prayer out loud, you also got extra points, so Baby tried once.

She said, "God, nobody knows who I am. If you know who I am, please come down and show me. I'd like to see if you're real anyway. Amen."

She got sent to the headmaster's office for that. The man at the big desk was the very same Father Michael she had thought was just a priest. He told Baby that he had come from an old California mission that had been deemed unsafe for services and closed down. "The parish that supports this school already had a fine young man to do the priestly duties," he informed her.

"And what are those?" she asked, curious about this new kind of school.

"He says Mass, hears confessions, offers the sacraments, you know, Catholic duties."

"What's a sacrament?"

"A service blessed by God."

"Can I get one?"

"Maybe when you're a little older."

"But then God can't bless me now," Baby persisted.

"Well, there are other ways to receive God's blessings, but the sacraments are the best."

"Who says?"

"History, my child, history," the priest said with a sigh. "But I think you're here to see me for doubting there is a God."

"I guess so."

"*Young lady, don't you know that God let his own son die for your sins?*" *Father Michael said.*

"*Why would he do that? Besides, I don't sin. I'm a good girl.*"

"*Everyone sins, and they are all the same in the eyes of God; no one's sins are better or worse than another's.*"

"*Well, I don't believe that. I could tell you a bad, bad sin that would make you cry. It's a sin God should never have let happen,*" *Baby told him.*

"*What's that, my child?*"

"*Someplace in Nevada, a little girl was stolen from her mother. The mother is suffering, and her daughter is lost, maybe dead. Tell me how God is going to fix that sin.*"

"*I don't have all the answers, child. Only God does.*"

"*Well, I wish he'd give some to me.*"

"*Read Romans 5:3–6, and see what you think.*"

"*Can I do a report on it for points?*"

"*I'd like that,*" *Father Michael said.*

"*If I get enough points, can I skip to seventh grade?*"

"*My, you are a direct young person. Can we continue this later? Aren't you late for your next class?*"

"*Where is the Isaiah building?*" *she asked.*

The sympathetic priest pointed the way, and soon she was flying through her fractions and anxious to get permission to approach the big bookcase in the fifth grade math room. She noticed a shelf that might have Bibles and took the chance to leave her seat.

"*Where do you think you're going?*" *a harsh voice said.*

"*Can I look at the books?*" *Baby asked.*

"*After your fraction exercises.*"

"*I finished them.*"

"*Then turn the page and do the multiplication and division problems.*"

"*Oh, I already did those … for fun,*" *she said.*

"*Who are you?*" *the stern, fifth grade math teacher, Phillip Wegner, asked.*

"*I don't know,*" *she said softly.*

◀◀◀◆▶▶▶

Later, in the motel room, she read Romans 5 from the Bible that had been placed in a drawer. It said— rejoice in our sufferings … *That was a weird idea. The little girl on the poster was not having fun. Maybe God can turn bad things into good. But here was a line*—hope does not disappoint us.

The next day before math, she slipped into Headmaster Michael's office. He was reading the Bible. He looked up and said, "Make it quick, sweetie. I don't want you to be late again."

"How can God turn bad things into good?"

"But that's already been done, child. When Jesus died on the cross, all the bad things people do were forgiven."

"I just can't believe that," Baby said adamantly.

"Maybe someday you will."

She shrugged her shoulders and hurried out. The bell was ringing when she rushed into Mr. Wegner's class. Hidden in her folder were some pages of algebra problems a ninth grader had showed her how to do. She would put those under her long division sheet when Mr. Wegner wasn't looking. She smiled when she thought how Mommy would never know the joy of solving an algebra equation.

But Mommy wanted to know that day how she liked the school.

"It's okay. School is school," she said.

"I mean the stuff about God. Is it interesting?"

She didn't answer right away and then said the only thing she knew. "We must rejoice in our sufferings."

"You're kidding," Mommy said. "Who says that?"

"The Bible," she answered. She started to reach for the Good Book where she had left it on the nightstand.

"No, no, no! You mean a person who is really suffering, *I mean suffering bad, will be joyful in the end?"*

"That's what it says … but I think some people suffer forever. There isn't enough joy in the world to make up for their suffering."

"Well, I think you're just getting too damn smart. Maybe we should change schools."

"I don't care … Can I take Dog for a walk?"

"Okay, but you'd better come right back or I'll show you both suffering you won't forget," Mommy warned. "Don't go out of my sight."

Baby walked around the small plot of grass in the courtyard of the motel. Her mind was spinning. The driveway opened toward a long street, the highway, and then the beach. Everything was jammed with cars and shoppers, strangers, frightening noises, and the unknown. Her heart began to run. Her legs stayed frozen to the spot, her leap for freedom stalled by the sound of Mommy's voice calling her back, the feel of Dog's nose against her hand, the thought of their suffering, the meaning of his name— Paradise.

◀◀◀◆▶▶▶

Around Christmas, Mr. Bowen tried to find Rainbow and Ellen Page. It was pretty clear they were no longer in Solvang, and, in fact, there were no Rainbows her age in public schools in California or Nevada. There were no driver's licenses issued to an Ellen Page with her height and hair color—he searched for brown, blonde, and red. He called the FBI and asked about a kidnapping at a fair someplace in Nevada. He was told, "Oh, that's a cold case." Mr. Bowen could hardly bear to say he'd seen a girl like the one on their posters and had let her slip away. Even though *he* hadn't seen the posters, Rainbow had, the truth written so plainly on her face. Then Mr. Bowen asked what the race of the abducted child was.

"Native American," came the crisp answer.

"Oh God," he whispered.

"Sir? Did you say something?"

"I'll get back to you," Mr. Bowen said and hung up.

The FBI recorded it as a crank call and did not inform the Roses.

8

◀◀◀◆▶▶▶

*I*n July, when Sunny turned twelve, something changed. She was often dizzy and disoriented. She couldn't remember things, and she slept a lot. Mommy put the protein powder in her juice two or three times a day, but she did not feel better. She moved slowly. She didn't have the strength to resist Mommy and hardly knew what the woman was doing. Sometimes she felt pain, but mostly she felt blank, like a baby who has to be fed and bathed and told what to do.

One morning, she wouldn't drink her juice. Mommy tried everything to get that juice down her, but Baby just said, "It's not cold enough … and it tastes funny."

"I'll make some ice cubes. You can finish it later," Mommy said.

That summer in California was the hottest on record. There were fires in the hills behind Santa Barbara, and once Ellen and Rainbow had to be evacuated from a motel close to the blaze. They wandered on the beach. Dog got to run a little but soon fell in step with them like an obedient child.

"Why don't you wear those shorts I bought you and get some tan on those pretty legs."

"I'm dark enough," Rainbow said.

"Are you defying me?"

"I don't even know what that means," the girl answered. She had always known more vocabulary words than anyone in her class at school. What was wrong with her?

Later, she was able to ditch the whole glass of juice in a plant by the front door without Mommy suspecting what she had done. A little fog lifted from her head.

The next day, when the sun raged overhead and they stayed in the motel room with the air-conditioning on high, Ellen said a strange thing. "I wonder how your father feels now."

Rainbow had never thought of a father. She had always had just a mommy.

"Who is my father?" Rainbow asked.

"Well, you'll never know that," Mommy said in a mean voice.

Rainbow had not imagined such a man, but when she did just then, she saw a handsome cowboy on a big horse reaching one hand down to, well … she didn't know what, but she was a small girl and carried a stuffed grey horse under her arm.

"What're you daydreamin' about now?" Mommy goaded.

"Oh, nothing. Going to Nevada someday."

"That's what you think!" Mommy said.

"Yeah. It's just a silly idea. I couldn't go without you, could I?"

"I should hope not! Let's get out of here. We need some groceries."

"I think I'll stay here," Rainbow said casually.

"I think not, Baby. What's gotten into you? I'm not fooling around."

"Haven't you had enough revenge?" Rainbow asked, the most daring thing she had ever said. Now that her brain was clearer, she was remembering things Mommy had said.

Mommy paused for a long time, as if trying to picture when she had told Baby such a thing. Then she laughed a raucous, heartless laugh. "As a matter of fact, no!" she said. She grabbed Baby's hand and pulled her out the door. "Dog can stay here in the nice cold air. You are coming with me. And you will never say the word Nevada again! Do you hear me?"

"Yes, Mommy."

They drove a few miles to a store on the outskirts of town, but there were a lot of cars in the parking lot because they were having some kind of farmer's market. There was no place to park away from the crowd like Mommy always did. She pulled between two trucks, so the smaller car was somewhat hidden, rolled up all the windows, and locked Baby to a metal ring she had installed on the floor board of the backseat, where Baby couldn't reach the door handles. "This is what Nevada feels like!" she said and left her there.

In thirty minutes, the temperature in the car had risen twenty degrees. Baby licked her own tears, but soon those were gone. Mommy didn't come back. She couldn't think. She didn't want to disappoint Mommy by doing something stupid. She was afraid of Mommy but depended on her for food and water and school. She wanted to be there when Mommy returned, being a good girl. But she didn't want to die.

She heard someone passing between Mommy's car and one of the trucks. She only hesitated a second. Then she screamed. Very quickly, things began to happen. A man began smashing a window and unlocking the door. Mommy would never forgive her for this. The man reached for her, and she shrank back, not wanting him to touch her. She heard sirens. She could breathe better now, but she was still hot. She would be okay when Mommy returned. She'd drink the thick juice with the protein powder and the ice cubes. She'd never say the word Nevada. She'd—

"What's your name, little girl?" another man asked. He had a gun on his belt.

"I'm called Baby, but I don't think it's my real name. Sometimes I'm called Rainbow."

"I won't hurt you ... Baby, but I need you to get out of the car."

"Mommy will be mad," she said, still unsure what to do.

"We'll talk to your mommy. She shouldn't have left you in this car all closed up."

"I'm not allowed to get out of the car," Baby said.

"I think this time it's okay," he said. He cut away the handcuffs.

Then there she was, coming out of the store with a huge cart brimming with wonderful things. Baby was so thirsty. She felt safe now and cried out, "Mommy! Mommy!"

The woman stopped short, saw the police cars and crowd around her car, around her child ... and she ran, pushing the metal basket at people trying to stop her. Some men in uniforms chased her, but Mommy was clever and disappeared behind a big truck. Baby was crying, "Mommy! Mommy!" A police woman made her get in one of the black and white *cars. She had a shiny badge and a smile on her Indian-looking face. Maybe she'd be nice like that lady who stopped Mommy for passing the school bus. Other men were searching Mommy's car. They were trashing Mommy's papers and clothes, and then they found a card under the front seat, an old credit card or something with a name on it—Liana.*

An officer opened the door where she sat terrified. "Is your mommy's name Liana?" he asked.

And from out of nowhere, clear as Nevada skies, she said, "No. My real mommy's name is Susan, Susan Rose. I don't live with her anymore."

◄◄◄◆►►►

When they got the phone call, Hank and Susan were sitting in the front porch swing watching the sun descend through striking golds and crimsons. It was Luz's night off, so Hank went in with some resignation. He cradled the phone. "Oh my God," he said. He leaned against the kitchen wall and stretched his hand toward his wife as she came into the room, still speaking into the phone, "Where? Where is she? Is she all right?"

Susan fell into his arms. Hank hung up and held her. "Sunny's alive. She's in California. Our daughter is alive," he said in a stunned voice.

"I don't believe it. Are they sure?"

"She told them her mother's name was Susan Rose. A woman left her in a locked car in a heat wave in Santa Barbara. She got away, but they know who she is." Hank drew his wife even closer. "This is the hard part, Susan," he said.

"Who? Who did this to us?"

Hank made her sit down at the oak table and went to the sink, letting the water run before pouring two glasses. He pulled a chair up as close to her as he could. Mostly he tried to give himself some time to figure out how to tell Susan what he had never talked about before. He had loved another woman, but she had almost broken him and his family, killed his dogs and stolen his grandmother's painting of the frightened colt that now hung over the fireplace in the living room. His father had found it at an art auction and returned it to its rightful place on the ranch. But Hank could hardly bare to think of *that* woman's hands on it.

He buried his head in his hands and then looked up and spoke a name he had not said in twenty years. "Liana."

"Liana?"

"She's someone from my past. I never told you because it was best forgotten," he said.

"You kept it from me? That you knew such a woman that could take our child?" she said.

"I'm so sorry, Susan. It was so long ago, long before I met you. I thought she was out of my life."

"But who is she?"

He tried to tell her about Liana in a way that wouldn't scare her, but the words felt like a flame in his throat, the sparks of Liana's behavior falling on his beautiful wife like pieces of some far-off conflagration—the killing of his dogs, the threats, the stealing of the painting, all landing against her bare heart with a blazing truth.

"She could have destroyed your whole family!"

"But she didn't. I had my eyes opened by a schizophrenic, my father's first wife. I learned something about forgiveness too. My folks gave forgiveness and more to his mentally ill ex-wife."

"I did hear something about that when I asked whose grave was out by Towering Peak, but this is different, Henry! This ... Liana ... stole more than a painting from us! She stole a whole span of Sunny's life. Of our lives! We have to go get our child! Now!"

"I'll call the airlines as soon as I hear from the psychiatrist," he said.

"The psychiatrist?"

He sighed. "Apparently there's some procedure in these cases."

"Cases? This is our daughter who's been missing for eight years! Procedures be damned!"

"They told me Sunny was having some problems."

"What problems?"

"With the disappearance of the person she's called Mommy all these years. With the fact that she's *our* daughter, people who might as well be strangers. This isn't going to be easy."

"Oh, Henry, how will we ever make it right?"

"I don't know. If only Julian and Serena were here. They would know what to do."

"Henry, what about the *round-pen* way? Sunny is a scared, abused—oh God, was she abused?"

"It's possible. They said she was suffering some physical trauma."

"I'll kill that woman, I swear I will!"

The ringing phone burst into their darkness.

"Henry Rose," Hank said into the receiver.

"Mr. Rose, this is Dr. Fielding, a psychiatric consultant for the Cottage Hospital in Santa Barbara. Thank God you've found your child!"

Hank pressed the speaker button and said, "My wife is listening now too. What shall we do?"

The doctor continued, "I suggest you wait a few days before you come see your daughter."

"No! We're coming tomorrow! I'm getting plane tickets now. Where is she?" he said, trying to control the emotion in his voice.

"Here at Cottage Hospital," he said.

"Can we speak to Sunny?" Susan asked calmly.

"Ah … she only responds to Baby, sometimes Rainbow, the names her kidnapper used."

"For God's sake, we thought she was dead," Hank snapped. "We need to hear her voice. This is just not real."

"I understand, Mr. Rose. We're doing everything possible for the child. She won't tell us much, just that they lived in a trailer or a motel most of the time. She doesn't want us to hurt the woman."

"Well, I'm going to wring the woman's neck if I ever see her again!" Hank said.

"Mr. Rose, I wouldn't be too hasty with my reactions right now," Fielding said. "And what did you mean, *see her again*?"

"I know the woman," Hank admitted.

"Really," the doctor said. "I think the police will be interested in that, and the FBI, of course."

"I'll do whatever it takes, talk to whomever I have to, but we're coming to Santa Barbara."

"I'll look forward to meeting you, Mr. Rose," Fielding said and broke the connection.

Susan and Hank went out to the barn and with one urgent motion gathered the wranglers around them. "Sunny's alive," Hank said in a choked voice. "Our daughter is alive."

Henry Dancing Horse looked into Susan's eyes and asked, "Who stole her?"

"You know, don't you?" she said.

"I think I do," he said.

"Liana," Susan told him.

"Yes. It had to be her. But damn, I didn't think of her when Sunny was kidnapped. By then Liana'd been gone for twenty years! How terrible for Hank. So much trouble, that woman. She has damaged two children. Have they caught her?"

"I don't know."

Hank held Susan with one arm and Dancing Horse with the other. Susan said to them, "I believed my baby was dead ... and now she's coming back ... no photos, no school records ... did she go to school? Why didn't she tell someone? She's been with *that* woman all this time. I can't bear it."

"Susan, stop," Hank pleaded.

"She would have obeyed her ... She would have been a good girl ... She wouldn't have cried," Susan went on between sobs.

Dancing Horse carried Susan back to the ranch house. Hank got on the phone immediately and bought the plane tickets. "We can get from Elko to Santa Barbara with a couple of stops ... tonight. We don't have much time."

"I'll drive you to the airport. What do you need?" Dancing Horse asked.

Susan spoke up from the couch where Dancing Horse had gently put her down. "Let's take some things she'll remember. Her dappled stuffed horse, Grey Boy, and that piece of obsidian you used to carry around."

"Okay. I'll pack those," Hank said.

"And maybe we should wear clothes she might remember. Can you still wear that leather jacket with the fringe?"

"I think so," he said.

◀◀◀◆▶▶▶

But it was not to be as simple as that. After several hours of traveling, changing planes, waiting in airports, and renting a car, they were not allowed to see their daughter. Sunny was heavily sedated. The doctors said she wouldn't let anyone touch her, and she kept asking for her mommy. They wanted the Roses to wait until the girl had some more rest. Two hours passed.

Finally, just as the sun rose after that long, long night, the psychiatrist, Dr. Fielding, told them Sunny was awake and asking about them. "That's good, right?" Hank said.

Fielding didn't give a very direct answer. "We'll see," he said.

When they got to her room, they decided Susan should go in alone carrying Grey Boy. Hank waited, tormented, outside the door.

◀◀◀◆▶▶▶

Baby looked up at the pretty, dark-skinned lady holding the stuffed horse. Her eyes were soft but anxious. Should she know her? She thought she had seen the horse. Yes, in her dream of her father.

"Grey Boy," the girl said.

"Yes. It's your Grey Boy," the lady said quietly and handed her the toy.

"Do I look like you?" Sunny asked.

"You do."

"Why?"

"Because I'm your mother," she said.

"Mommy?"

84

"No. I'm your *real* mother. You were taken from me when you were four years old."

Sunny looked away for a moment. "At the fair."

"Yes. You remember."

"I don't remember. It's just something I figured out … about that little girl who was kidnapped in Nevada."

"Sunny. You are that little girl."

"The girl on the poster?"

"You saw one of the posters?"

"A long time ago. Did I call you Mommy?"

"No, Sunny. You called me Momma."

"Then who is Mommy?"

"The kidnapper," the woman answered.

It all came together in Sunny's head, but it was painful. She wouldn't let the woman hold her.

"Is Daddy here?"

"Just outside."

"Daddy?" Sunny said in a louder voice. She seemed to be waking up from the drugs.

A man stepped through the door, and there was the cowboy she had imagined. He was real. He was her father. She let him hold her hand. He seemed nice, like Mr. Bowen. Suddenly, she looked around the room and gripped her father's hand tighter.

"What's your name?" she asked as if that might confirm some memory she had of him.

"Hank," he answered.

"Robert Henry Askay Rose," she said clearly.

"Yes! You remember!"

"Henry Four Names. Yes. But something's wrong. Something's missing," she said. She struggled in the blankets trying to get out of the bed. "Oh, oh, the dog! Where's the dog?"

"What dog?"

"Paraíso." She said Dog's name aloud for the first time, to people she didn't know. "He'll be hungry now," she whimpered.

"Oh my God," Hank whispered, not letting go of Sunny's hand.

"Mommy has a dog. When she first took me, it was a puppy. Now it's old and tired. I don't get to pet it much. She says I'll like the dog too much. I have to like her best. She wouldn't tell me his real name for a long time. I just called him Dog."

"Oh, my dear child, I am so sorry."

"Please save him, Daddy, please," Sunny begged.

"I will, Sunny, I promise."

"When Mommy and I were choosing fake names so I could go to school, I said I wanted to be called Sunny. I *am* Sunny? That's my real name?"

"Yes," Hank said, "Marta Serena Sun Rose."

"Oh, I like that," she said.

Her mother moved closer to the bed. "Can I stay with you while Daddy looks for Paraíso?"

"Okay. I don't like being alone. It might get too hot. I might suffocate. I might need someone … to open the window."

She was drifting on the sedatives but being such a good girl and not crying. Mommy would be proud of her. She wondered why Mommy had run away. She didn't mean for anyone to break the window on the car. She moaned with guilt. And then her mother put her hand on her forehead.

"You're almost home, Sunny. You'll be in Nevada. You'll ride the big Grey Boy. You'll be our daughter again."

These words comforted her as she lay on the edge of consciousness, although she wasn't sure what all of them meant.

"Nevada," she whispered. "Nevada … Nevada." And then she dropped into a dark but healing place.

◀◀◀◆▶▶▶

Hank went to the Santa Barbara Humane Society first. He recognized Paraíso immediately when he walked down the cement aisles past the kennels. The dog had that black face with small scuffs of brown on his ears and neck, just like the one Liana had taken the night they broke up. Of course, it wasn't the same dog, but he could be related to the ones buried at the ranch. And Liana had given him one of the same names. *Oh, what a twisted heart*, Hank thought.

The attendant said, "We got a call yesterday from the manager at Motel 6 about a barking dog in one of the rooms. The lady had left without paying a month's rent, and then the dog had pretty much destroyed the place."

"Can I have him now?" Hank asked.

"Well, there's the motel bill. We're not supposed to release him."

"I'll pay it. Call them up. I can't leave this dog here. He's been through hell, and my daughter is in the hospital waiting for him. Please," Hank pleaded.

Hank made the arrangements and went out with the dog trotting happily beside him, nudging his leg now and then to reaffirm the presence of this man who had come for him. Hank stopped before they reached the rental car and threw his arms around Paraíso, believing him to be the grandson or great-grandson of his own female Paraíso, the one Liana had poisoned years ago. The beautiful dog licked his face and gazed in Hank's eyes as if he knew him. The dog was old, but now he would have the love he had been missing for his whole life. "Thank you for being my daughter's friend," he told the dog. Paraíso wagged his tail.

Hank walked right in the hospital with Paraíso. "Don't try to stop me," he said to anyone who approached with disapproval. By now Sunny's story had spread, so no one deterred him. Sunny was asleep with Susan holding one of her hands when Hank led the shepherd up to the bed. The dog put both paws up on the fresh sheets and licked the girl's face. She opened her eyes and kissed the dog, exclaiming, "Paraíso! Paraíso!" She looked at her father. "You found him!"

"Yes. He's all right."

"Did you find Mommy?"

"No, Sunny. The police are still looking."

"They won't find her. No one would have found me, but the car was on fire, and I had to scream."

"You did the right thing, Sunny. Do you think you can come home with us?"

"You mean to Nevada?"

"Yes. Your mother and I have prayed for this day for eight years."

"I don't remember you very well."

"Do you remember Grey Boy?" Susan asked.

"This one?" Sunny said, holding up the stuffed toy.

"No, the real one."

"I have a real horse?" Sunny asked.

"He's old now but still healthy. Wouldn't you like to see him?"

"Can Mommy come?" She squirmed under the covers.

A short, heavyset nurse whose name tag said Cedra came in just then. "Maybe that's enough for today, Mr. Rose. She's been through a lot," the woman suggested.

"We can't just leave her!"

"Of course not. You can stay in town until she's released and, of course, questioned by the FBI."

"Haven't they already done that?" Susan asked.

"She wouldn't give them very much at the time they picked her up. She might reveal more now that she feels safe."

"It seems to me she'll feel safer with her parents in the room than alone with strangers," Hank said.

"You're strangers too in many ways," Cedra reminded them. "Give me your number. I'll call if she needs you, okay?"

Sunny had fallen back asleep, but when they tried to leave, the dog wouldn't budge.

"The dog could be a problem," the nurse said.

"He thought he'd lost her forever, just like we did. Can't he stay for a while?" Hank asked.

"I suppose. I like dogs. I'll keep an eye on him," she said.

The Roses went out into the hallway. Dr. Fielding met them at the door. "I believe there are some things you should know," he said. "Can we talk in my office?"

"This doesn't sound good," Hank said.

"It could be worse, I suppose," the doctor said. "I believe you two being here will help in the long run, but you need to have all the information."

They sat down in Dr. Fielding's office and waited while he gathered some papers and other materials. Then he began. "There's no easy way to prepare you for this, but your daughter has been sexually molested. I don't know for how long but probably off and on the entire eight years."

"Oh God," Hank said.

"What did that woman do?" Susan asked.

"The child has scars from tearing and battering in the vaginal area and bruises around her breasts. Those are very recent. When we asked her about these injuries, she just said, 'Mommy liked to keep me very clean.' When we asked if Mommy ever hurt her, she said she didn't remember, that she tried to be a good girl and do what Mommy wanted, so she could go to school. She said there were never any men involved in their lives, so that's some comfort. Usually with women abusers, there's not the violence that men exhibit. It would be very confusing to the child nevertheless. I advise extreme caution in this area."

"What do you mean?" Susan asked.

"You should not touch her at all, unless she initiates it, especially in those sensitive areas. Answer all her questions as reasonably as you can. Stockholm syndrome may apply here. As you may know that—"

"I know what it means," Hank interrupted.

Fielding continued. "Let her call the woman Mommy. Don't ask her why she didn't run away or seek help. There's usually deep psychological control imposed by the abductor, especially since the girl was taken at such a young age. It was a random snatching, I assume. We'll know more when they've apprehended the kidnapper."

"That's where you're wrong, sir," Hank said. "It wasn't random at all."

"What?"

"I told you earlier that I knew the woman. She abused me when I was twelve years old. When I was seventeen, my mother devised a way for me to get out of the relationship. Liana vanished. I should have known she could have done this. I should have prepared for it."

"I am truly shocked, Mr. Rose. How painful it must be for you and your wife, having to bring up these past … situations. I don't think Sunny should know about this."

"I won't lie to her," Hank said.

"It's your decision, of course," Dr. Fielding said, "but these things take time."

"We've lost eight years with our daughter. We don't want to lose a second more," Hank said adamantly.

"She's not the little girl who was taken from you. Can you accept her as she is?" the doctor asked.

"That will never be a problem," Hank said.

"She may not be a little girl, but she's still our daughter," Susan added.

Hank's cell phone rang. He stepped outside the room.

An FBI agent said, with barely an introduction, "Mr. Rose? She came back for the dog. We got 'er!"

"Where is she?" Hank asked.

"Santa Barbara Police have her in custody, but since it's a kidnapping, we'll resume command, and she'll be arraigned in a federal court."

"I want to see her," Hank said.

"Now's your best chance, before she gets a lawyer."

Hank left Susan with their sleeping child and drove to the police station. He felt sick. How could he face her? What would he say? This was worse than a nightmare because it was so real. He told his mother that he *loved* this woman when Serena was waving all kinds of red flags in front of him. He had sex with this woman who now, maybe, probably, did … something like that to his child! Oh God. He barely got the car stopped outside the station before he opened the door and threw up in the gutter at the curb. He didn't feel any better.

He went inside the building and told the officer at the desk who he was. The man raised his eyebrows and picked up a set of keys. "Do you want to go in with her?"

"No," Hank said, wondering where the bathroom was. "I just need to tell her something."

"Is your little girl okay?" the officer asked.

"Not yet," Hank said.

The two men walked down a long aisle with cells on either side. They were full.

"Mostly drunks," the sergeant explained. "Probably gone tomorrow. I hear the woman is going to Federal."

"Yes," Hank said. "She'll never get out."

Then he was standing before her. He couldn't believe what he saw—a blonde woman in heels so high, she seemed a half a foot taller than he remembered, dirty clothes on an unrecognizable body. He knew the blonde hair was a wig. He almost wanted to see the curls of red framing her still faintly attractive face. This was a stranger.

But he grabbed the bars with renewed anger. "Liana!" he said.

She whirled around, surprise in her eyes. She cried out to him as he neared the cell, "Robert Henry Askay Rose! What do you think of yourself now? Your perfect life!"

"I think I was the world's worst fool. How could you, Liana? How could you hurt my daughter?"

"Oh, I didn't hurt her. She enjoyed every minute of it!" Liana taunted.

Hank had no words for that. He couldn't even imagine the fear and pain his daughter must have endured, the waiting for someone to rescue her. His gut rolled, but he wouldn't give Liana the satisfaction of seeing him clutch his stomach.

He wanted to hit her, but he went on with as much determination in his voice as he could muster. "I only came to say one thing. I am not my father. I will never forgive you."

He remembered the day Julian came into Miranda's hospital room in her prison mental ward and said, "I forgive you." Hank was filled anew with admiration and love for a man that could do that.

"I'll never forgive you," he said again.

She leaned closer to the bars and said, "But you'll never forget me."

"Probably not. But I will get back what you took from me. I got the dog. I got my grandmother's painting too."

"How the hell did you do that?" she asked.

"It's a long story, and I don't plan to be here that long," he said.

"It got me a few bucks, anyway. But it didn't satisfy me. I wanted something you cared enough about to give your *life* for!"

"Well, you got that, damn you. Are you happy now?"

"I'll be happy when that Baby starts talking to you! I mean really *talking* to you. I just wish I could be a fly on the wall," she said. Then she twirled around the cell with a heartless laugh condemning the very air. "You won't forget me, little Hank."

Hank turned away and moved quickly through the room. Liana screamed as if wanting the last word more than anything as he bolted from the specter of his past, "You'll never forget me!"

◄◄◄◆►►►

When Hank returned to the hospital, Sunny was fully awake. She was holding onto Paraíso's collar with a wild look in her eyes. "Please don't take him! Please," she pleaded with anyone who came near him.

"Sunny," Hank said, "if you'll let the nurse have him for a while, I'll tell you about … Mommy."

"You found her?" the girl said, letting go of the dog.

Nurse Cedra had offered to take him for a walk on her break that was just coming up. She led him gently away. Paraíso whined and strained at the leash, but she finally got the dog out the door.

"You found Mommy?" Sunny asked again

"The police did. She's in jail."

"Noooo! She didn't hurt me. I was a bad girl sometimes. It wasn't her fault. She took good care of me," Sunny cried.

What had the psychiatrist said? *She'll deny the abuse as long as she can.*

"Sunny, that woman took you from us at the fair almost eight years ago," Hank said as calmly as he could.

"No! That was that other girl!" Sunny insisted.

"What other girl?" her mother asked.

"The girl on the poster. The girl from Nevada."

"Oh Lord, Sunny. You saw the poster?" Hank had not heard this yet.

"Yes. A long time ago, years ago. I felt so bad for her. Did they find her?"

Hank wanted to gather his daughter in his arms and never let go. And never answer that question, but he said, "Yes. They found her."

"Was she okay?" Sunny asked. There was some excitement in her voice, and she sat up straighter in the bed.

"She was alive, but she was not okay. She had been abused by the kidnapper."

Sunny reacted like she'd been hit, but whatever she recognized, she immediately rejected.

"I have to tell Mr. Bowen!" she said.

"Who's Mr. Bowen?" Susan asked.

"My third grade teacher up in Solvang. I told him about the girl on the poster when we were studying Nevada. We had to do some homework, find out something interesting about Nevada that wasn't in our book. I got an A that day. He'll want to know what happened to her. Please call him, Daddy."

Hank loved the sound of that last word. "I'll do that right now … and I'll bring Paraíso back."

"Oh, thank you, Daddy!"

He was earning her trust, but at what cost?

◄◄◄◆►►►

It was seven o'clock in the evening. Hank didn't expect to find Bowen's number easily, as he thought most teachers had unlisted numbers, but there it was in the Solvang directory—Allen Bowen. He punched in the number. A woman answered, "Yes?"

"May I speak to Mr. Bowen?"

"Who's calling?"

"The father of one of his former students, a girl named Serena Sun Rose."

Hank could hear the woman telling the teacher this. He had no idea what to expect. He could hardly believe Liana had allowed Sunny to go to school.

A man's voice came on the line. "That name doesn't sound familiar. How many years ago did I have her in my class?"

"I don't know for sure, maybe three," Hank said.

"Mr. Rose, I'll need to know more."

"All I know, Mr. Bowen, is that my daughter said she told you a story in class about a girl who was abducted in Nevada, that she and her mommy had seen the girl's picture on a poster."

"Oh my god … Rainbow!"

"Rainbow?"

"She was introduced to me as Rainbow. She looked Native American. The name fit. She was very smart. We all thought she should be skipped a grade, but the mother wouldn't consider it. She was here through fourth grade, and then she and her mother sort of disappeared. I always wondered what happened to her. I even drove up the highway on spring break to see those posters for myself but never found any. I thought Rainbow was so clever to have made that all up, I let it go."

"Mr. Bowen, those posters were taken down that year, because the child had been missing since she was four years old. She must have been nine or ten then. That child is my daughter, Sunny."

"But you found her?"

"Yes. The woman who kidnapped her called herself Ellen Page."

"God in heaven, Rainbow's mommy! Rainbow was the girl on the poster! Mr. Rose, I have to tell you, she came to me after class once and said, 'That girl was taken from a fair.' I asked her how she knew that, and she said, 'It's a secret.' You have to understand, I hear everything from third graders. I do remember telling her fourth grade teacher that I felt she was a child at risk. What can I do, Mr. Rose? I really let you folks down."

"Mr. Bowen, would you come to Santa Barbara and see Sunny? She needs to make some connections on her own with people she trusts. I think you could help."

"I'll definitely come. I'll come tomorrow. Is there anything else I should know?"

"Yes. She was sexually abused for years, but she doesn't know what that means. We're all tiptoeing around the subject. I believe you were a bright spot in her life. She may be able to come to terms with what happened to her if there were bright spots along the way."

"How old is she?"

"Twelve."

Mr. Bowen was silent for a moment and then said, "You know, I called the FBI about that poster. They said it was a cold case, but I knew something wasn't right. How could I have missed this, this terrible thing staring me in the face?"

"Mr. Bowen, we all missed things." Hank was reminded of the phone call from the child in Winnemucca and the woman with the German shepherd that had been Liana after all. "We can only pray for a sane future for our daughter. She's in Cottage Hospital, room 206."

"I'll be there in the morning," the teacher agreed.

◀◀◆▶▶

Paraíso stayed by Sunny's bed. She allowed him to go out for walks because Mr. Bowen was on his way to see her. He made her life real, but it was not the *real* she needed now. When that would come was anybody's guess. Before Hank and Susan said good night, she asked them, "Why am I in the hospital?"

Susan told her the doctors said she was malnourished and emotionally stressed, that supervised rest was the best thing for her.

"I'm sort of tired of being *supervised*," she said.

"We're going to take you home as soon as possible," her father said.

"Home?"

"To Nevada."

"Okay. I … I like Nevada, but I don't know why."

"You'll remember when we get there," Hank promised her.

◀◀◆▶▶

The Roses decided to go a nearby motel. On their way out of the hospital, they faced a barrage of faces, mostly reporters. Many townspeople who had read about the kidnapping and recovery of

Sunny Rose offered their homes as a refuge from the press, a place they could rest, have meals, but Hank said to one couple that seemed to have too much interest in the situation, "I think my wife and I would like to be alone. We're exhausted."

Hank walked with hunched shoulders, barely able to support Susan. They reached the rental car and crawled gratefully into the private space, but they didn't say a word to each other until they were in the motel room and had had a comforting drink of cold Mountain Dew from the vending machine down the hall.

Then Susan broke the silence. "What did you say to that … Liana?"

"I told her I'd never forgive her."

"That's good," Susan said.

"It didn't help," Hank said.

"Are you going to see her again?"

"I hope not. The next time, I might get my hands around her neck … but I don't really want to touch her," Hank said. "I should be on my knees thanking God that Sunny's alive, but I'm so sick about what Liana might have done to her, besides imprisoning her for eight years, that I can't eat or sleep or even think straight."

He didn't tell her that he had really *been* sick at the police station. She had too much to worry about.

"We should be asking the Great Spirit to heal our child. Our feelings don't matter," Susan said.

"We should have found her sooner, but we have to learn how to help her now. We can't expect God to do everything," Hank said.

"I'm worried about the FBI questioning Sunny more," Susan admitted.

"Me too, but they need to build their case against Liana. They have to know everything that woman did to her."

"I don't think she'll tell them."

"I don't think so, either. Does she even know? She was so young. Maybe she'll remember the recent stuff, but those years before she went to school? They're probably a blur," Hank said.

"We have to be there," Susan said.

"We will," Hank promised.

They took their shoes off and lay on top of the covers on the soft bed. Hank pulled a light blanket over them, and they rested but did not sleep. Hank had a dull ache behind his eyes that was threatening to become a severe headache. Susan reached over without him saying a word and caressed his forehead with her cool fingers.

"You are so much like my mom," Hank said.

"She taught me many things about her men, how they do not like to talk about their pain but are heartened by the smallest relief."

"I love you," Hank whispered.

"As I love you," she said.

◀◀◀◆▶▶▶

When the Roses returned to the hospital a while later, there were FBI agents and doctors outside Sunny's room. Dr. Fielding pointed to something on Sunny's chart and said, "Hank. Susan. I'm glad you're here. Sunny's blood work has shown a slight infection, but she's not feeling too bad. I've told these people to wait a day or two, but they're insisting on an interview with your daughter now."

"The longer we wait to question her, the more difficult it will be for her to remember details," the woman with the ID badge reading *Sally Soprano* said.

"We want to be with her," Hank insisted.

"I'm afraid that might compromise what she says," the other detective weighed in.

"I don't like it either," Dr. Fielding said, "but there is an intercom where you'll be able to hear everything."

The investigators explained that they wanted to approach Sunny together, but only one of them would stay when they determined with whom she was the most comfortable. As Hank and Susan took in this information, Roger Halford said, "I think she'd rather talk to a man since the abductor was female."

The woman detective disagreed. "It's the person she trusts the most that she'll open up to, the person whose behavior doesn't scare

97

her. We have to be very sensitive to what she's been through," Sally said.

The two FBI agents entered Sunny's room. The shepherd growled. "It's okay, Paraíso," Sunny said. "They just want to help me."

The man began. "I'm Detective Halford. What's your name, young lady?"

"Rainbow."

"Just Rainbow?"

"I think so." Sunny twisted the sheets in her hands.

The woman said, "You can call me Sally, Rainbow. Now, did anyone ever call you anything else?"

"Mommy called me Baby for a long time, but she didn't think that was a good school name, so we made up names like a game. I was called Rainbow. Mr. Bowen remembers. He's coming to see me today. He can tell you what a good girl I was."

"You're not in trouble, Sunny. May I call you Sunny?" the woman detective asked in a gentle voice.

"I guess so. When Mommy and I were playing the game, I said I wanted the name Sunny, but she got very angry. She said that was a silly name, and I couldn't ever have that name. I kind of got used to Rainbow. It felt like a grown-up name. When she called me Baby, bad things would happen. I don't want to talk about that."

Those were the most sentences she had strung together since she'd been found.

"What was your mommy's name?" the man asked.

"Ellen Page."

"Did you know that wasn't your *real* mommy?" he asked in a rougher tone.

"Sometimes," Sunny answered, pulling the covers up almost over her mouth.

The woman signaled to her partner, and he left. Then she said, "Well, it doesn't matter *who* she was, because you *thought* it was your real mommy. Did she tell you your parents didn't want you? That they gave you to *her* to raise?"

"No."

"Are you sure?"

"I'm sure."

"What did she tell you?"

"She said she had a puppy I might want to see, that Daddy wanted me to see it."

"And was there a puppy?"

"Yes."

"What was his name?

"Dog."

At this, Paraíso cocked his ears, and before the woman continued, Sunny offered, "That wasn't his real name. His name was Paraíso, but Mommy didn't tell me because she didn't think I'd understand it. It's Spanish."

"Yes, I know," the woman said. "How old was the puppy?"

"He was a big puppy, so I guess Mommy lied about that part. We called him Dog right away."

"How old are you?"

"The doctor told me I was twelve."

"Hmm … eight years. You were with Mommy for quite a while. What's the first thing you remember being with her?"

"I was chained with Dog in the back of a kind of truck with no windows. It was cold and dark."

"What happened to the puppy?"

"He's right here. I told you."

"*This* is that puppy?" the woman said with disbelief.

"Yes. This is Paraíso."

"That's an odd name for a dog," the detective said. "How did Mommy think of that name?"

"She said she'd tell me someday, but she never did."

"Well, okay … now about names. Do you know what Mommy's real name is?"

Outside, Hank grabbed Dr. Fielding's arm. "She doesn't need to know that yet. There are things only I can tell her. You have to stop this!"

"No," Sunny said.

"You lived with this woman for eight years and never heard her real name?"

Hank was fuming. "You'd better stop this, or I'll make a scene this hospital will never forget!"

Dr. Fielding went into the room and motioned the investigator into a corner. "You'll just confuse the child. Please take a different line of questioning."

"I'm just trying to establish the family connection."

"And the family can do that, if they wish, at a later time. I insist."

Hank relaxed a little but moved closer to the intercom outside Sunny's room so he could hear anything she said about Liana. Susan stared at her husband. He knew the connection to *that* woman was something his wife *never* wanted Sunny to know.

Inside with Sunny, Sally Soprano pressed on.

"All right, Sunny, what's the next thing you remember?"

Sunny glanced out the window at the flame-red bougainvillea lining the entrance and the blue sky beyond.

"Being hungry," she said.

"Did Mommy kiss you good night?"

"No."

"Did Mommy touch you?"

"No."

"Did you play games?"

"Like what?"

"Cards or checkers or twenty questions?"

"No."

"What did you do all the time?"

"Look for places to park or a motel when we needed … baths."

Sunny said this last word with great hesitation.

"Did Mommy undress you?"

"No. Never."

"Did Mommy wash you?"

This got a stunned silence from the child.

"I don't remember," she said.

Dr. Fielding didn't need Hank to prod him this time. He went in the room saying, "That's enough, Detective. This will get you nowhere. There are things she doesn't remember and can't tell you."

Sunny looked straight at the FBI woman and said, "I do remember Mommy liked me to be very, very clean."

And the interview was over.

Almost at that moment, Mr. Bowen came down the hospital corridor with a tidy, prettily-dressed woman by his side. "Mr. and Mrs. Rose?" he said as he reached Hank and Susan.

"Yes," Hank said.

"I'm Allen Bowen, and this is my wife, Cynthia."

"Oh, I'm so glad you came just now," Hank said, grasping the man's hand.

Immediately, Cynthia asked Susan if she would like someone to talk to, and they went off together toward the lounge.

"Thank you, Mr. Bowen, for coming so quickly," Hank said.

"Allen, please. Now where is your daughter?"

"Right in here."

The two of them entered Sunny's room.

"Mr. Bowen!" she cried.

"My little Rainbow, you're all grown up!"

"Now you can make everyone believe me!"

"Of course. What would you like them to believe?"

"I knew about the girl on the poster. I knew Nevada was important."

"Maybe they haven't gotten that far in their questioning."

"But it's important. It's the first time I knew something on my own, something Mommy didn't tell me, something that wasn't made up, something that wasn't a lie!"

"What did you know about that girl?"

"I knew it was me!"

Hank wondered how long she had really known that and if Liana had seen that poster and gone deeper into hiding. It didn't seem to him that Santa Barbara was a very smart place to hide.

"Why didn't you tell me, Rainbow?"

She looked away from his honest eyes.

"Because I didn't want Mommy to hurt me. I wanted to go to school. She said I could go to school if she could make me clean all over, especially clean inside."

There, in a few minutes, Mr. Bowen had learned more from Sunny than all the detectives and doctors that had been with her for days.

"Oh, Rainbow, I wish you had told me this back then."

"I know. Me too. But I was scared."

"But you can go home now, with your real parents and start over again."

"I can go home, Mr. Bowen, but I can never start over."

◀◀◀◆▶▶▶

In the waiting room, Cynthia Bowen sat holding Susan's hand. "This is just a terrible, terrible thing, Mrs. Rose. I can't say I fully know what you're feeling, because Allen and I have no children, but if you need to talk or cry or hit something, just do it. I'm here for you," she said.

For the first time, Susan felt she could let her defenses down. Mrs. Bowen looked at her so eagerly and sincerely.

"She's not my child," Susan said softly. "I mean, not the child I lost. I didn't see her grow or lose her first tooth or send her off for her first day of school. She's a stranger to me. I … I don't even feel love for her … yet. Is there something wrong with me?"

"No, no, Mrs. Rose … Susan. You missed those things with her, but … well, I hope I'm not overstepping … you missed all the other bad things that could have happened if she hadn't been kidnapped and the bad things that did happen. It wasn't fair, but you were spared some horrible things, so now you can bring all the good things back into her life. You can give her all the things that awful woman could never give her—a family, horses, education, friends, maybe a church, her own room in a safe house. Oh, just think what you can do now! You can be her real mother, something she needs more than anything. Your love for her will come back."

"Oh, I don't think I'll ever be enough for her. How can I erase what that woman has done?"

"You can't erase it, I guess, but you can help her forget. You can give her new memories that are better than the old ones."

Susan thought about that. "I like that. But what if she doesn't want those things? What if she's locked in that eight-year world and doesn't need the things she missed in our world, the normal world?"

"She'll want them, Mrs. Rose. I'll bet anything she'll want them."

"Well, I know one thing, Mrs. Bowen. Your husband was the first *good* thing that happened to her in that other world. I thank him with all my heart. If she can remember something good from that time, maybe she'll accept something good from *this* time."

"Something good will come, I'm sure of it," Cynthia said and gave Susan a hug.

◄◄◄◆►►►

Dr. Fielding sedated Sunny when Bowen went too far and told the girl he had looked for the posters and couldn't find them, because they'd all been taken down. It was innocent enough. She had asked him if he knew what happened to the posters, and he thought he should tell her the truth.

"They took the posters down? They stopped looking for me? They let Mommy scrub me raw and slap me and starve me and leave me in a burning car?"

She was near hysteria by then, and Dr. Fielding had no choice. Allen Bowen left the room defeated, but the doctor came out and said to Mr. Bowen and to Hank, "No one can predict what will set her off. Don't worry that you'll say something wrong. In fact, I believe Sunny needs to realize events like this to really get over what was done to her, to blame the perpetrator, not herself or others."

Hank and Allen went toward the lounge. Mr. Bowen tried to assure Hank that his wife had a way of comforting people, but Hank saw the anxiety rise in Susan when he told her that their daughter had to be sedated again. Her eyes got wild, and she held her hand tightly to her mouth.

"It was actually a kind of breakthrough," Hank explained to calm his wife. "Sunny couldn't stand to think the posters were gone. She feels betrayed, I'm sure, but may be beginning to feel the truth about 'Mommy' and who she herself is. Too bad the FBI people weren't in there since they were the ones who removed the damn things!"

Nurse Cedra came down the hall with Paraíso and handed Hank the leash. "He needs to go out," she said.

The Roses and the Bowens went out of the hospital. They walked in silence to a small park nearby. The German shepherd raced around the green lawn and circled his new friends gleefully. Then he lay at their feet to rest a little. Finally, Mr. Bowen said, "I'll bet the dog knows a thing or two." He didn't mean it to be funny, but suddenly they were all laughing at the absurdity of it. It felt freeing to see the humorous side in the face of nameless terrors and regrets.

9

◀◀◀◆▶▶▶

"Liana? Mommy? Ellen?"

The kidnapper looked at her court-appointed lawyer with a blank face.

"Miss Page? Whoever you are, you listening to me?"

"No. I was thinking about the dog. That was a good dog."

"Well, apparently he's with the Roses now and okay. What about the child?"

"She was bad, mostly bad."

"I mean, did you know what you were doing when you took her?"

"You bet I did," Liana said.

"Had you been drinking or doing drugs?"

"Hell, no!"

"Did you think about the consequences of your actions?"

"No again." She smiled. "I got my consequences. They got theirs."

"I'm trying to get you off on insanity," the frustrated lawyer said.

"I'm not insane, so forget that."

"Did you sexually abuse the child?"

"No way. She'll tell you. I just kept her little body clean. There's nothing wrong with that."

"She'll have to accuse you of specific sexual acts to make a charge of abuse stick."

"Well, it's her word against mine, isn't it. Kids lie all the time."

"They have a witness that says he told another person your child was at risk."

"Who's that?"

"A schoolteacher named Mr. Bowen."

"Oh, that nerd. He doesn't know anything."

"I'm afraid that's not entirely true. I've been informed he's seen the girl and got her to say she knew she was the girl on the poster."

"That damn poster! Of all the places we went, what're the chances Baby would see that? And she couldn't even read really."

"Apparently she read the words *Nevada* and *Reward.*"

"Yeah, I guess I was insane enough to teach her how to read!"

"You kidnapped a child. You crossed two state lines that we know of, and you, maybe, molested her. How do you think that'll go over with a jury?"

"Hey, I kept them jumping for eight years. I don't care what you do to me."

"Kidnapping is a capital offense. Do you know what that means?"

"Do I care?"

"You could get the death penalty."

Liana was silent then, twisted a little in her handcuffs, and finally said, "I'm just sorry they got the dog."

◄◄◄◆►►►

Hank and Susan were there when Sunny woke up. She seemed glad to see them. "It's not that I don't remember you," she said right away, "but that I don't know you … and you don't know me."

"We've thought of that, Sunny," her father said, "so we're going to start fresh. Do you want to be called Rainbow?"

"No. I like Sunny. I like my whole name. They told me. Marta Serena Sun Rose. I like it very much. And I remember Grey Boy. I definitely want to keep him. Did we go to church when I was little?"

"Once in a while, on special occasions," Susan said.

"Mommy and I never went to church, but I read the Bibles in the motel rooms after Mommy threw out some of my books when I was bad. And last year I went to Catholic school. Father Michael and I would talk about different ideas. He was nice. We could go to church. That would be a new thing."

"We could definitely do that," Susan said, "and I could teach you the Native American spiritual way. You are half Iroquois."

"I don't feel like a Native American. I don't feel like a twelve-year-old. I don't know what it means to be in the real world."

"We'll help you, Sunny. Trust us," Hank said.

"I want to trust you, but I have questions."

"Try one," he said.

"Why did you let Mommy take me away from the fair?"

"We each thought the other had a hold of your hand," Susan admitted.

"Oh."

"It's our fault," Hank said. "It's all our fault."

"I just wanted to see the puppy. It's my fault too. I made a mistake."

"Sunny, your mother and I made plenty of mistakes, but from now on will you help us find our daughter again?"

"What if I can't tell you … things?"

"Well, we have an idea about that. We're going to buy you some blank posters that you can nail up different places on the ranch, like on our bedroom door, on the greenhouse wall, or on the arena railing. You can write what you want to tell us. We'll really *see* you, what's in your heart. We'll *find* you this time, find you in the way that you needed to be found for years," Hank finished.

"That's the nicest thing anyone has ever done for me. Except one time a lady put me behind her on her horse and rode into the ocean. That was fantastic. I got punished later though. I may not have to use the posters forever." She paused. "Momma?"

Susan flushed at the word. "Yes, Sunny."

"Thank you for saving Paraíso and bringing Mr. Bowen to see me. I will be a good girl from now on."

"May I kiss your cheek, Sunny?" Susan asked.

"That would be okay." And Hank saw the girl just flinch ever so slightly before she said, "I'm ready to go home now."

Dr. Fielding gave the Roses some medications for their daughter and provided the name of a good psychiatrist in a small town fairly close to the ranch. Hank asked him, "How will we know when to use these?" holding up the bottles full of pills.

"You can always call me, but I think the signs will be there. Let Sunny tell you what she needs, about more than meds. You understand," he said.

Sunny came out of her room just then, dressed in the clothes she was recovered in—too small, out of style, and raggedy. "Do you think I could have something else to wear home?" she asked.

"What would you like?" her mother asked as Hank glanced at the return tickets and said they had plenty of time.

"Oh, I want a dressage outfit!" she cried.

"That should be easy to find in Santa Barbara," Susan said.

In a couple of hours, they had bought so much besides riding clothes, Hank had to find a luggage store and purchase a suitcase. Sunny seemed to enjoy the shopping adventure until in one dress shop, a sales woman with long, red curls came toward them. Sunny shrank behind her father and begged to leave. Hank knew then that her healing was tentative, at best.

When they got to the airport and prepared to board, Sunny said, "Flying on an airplane. A first, huh, Daddy?"

To get home the quickest, least stressful way for Sunny and Paraíso, Hank had to find three seats on a semiprivate commuter jet with one stop. Thank God he had the kind of money to do that. He had to put the dog in a carrier in the cargo hold but was told he'd be allowed to see him at the scheduled stop. It was a clear day, and the pilot told Hank he didn't expect much turbulence.

"This your daughter's first flight?" the young pilot asked.

"Sure is," Hank told him.

They boarded, and soon the turboprop streamed down the runway and lifted off in a sharp angle from the ground. When the plane made a sweeping turn out over the Pacific Ocean, going west and then east, Sunny said to her parents from the window seat, "I'll miss the ocean. I really liked its sound, its immensity. I'll never forget the lady on the beach who let me ride behind her on her horse right into the waves. Mommy just about had a heart attack!"

"What kind of a horse was it?" Susan asked.

"I don't know. It was big, and it was a chestnut. I remember wondering why I knew that color."

"A good friend of yours at home has a chestnut," Susan reminded her.

"Dancing Horse?"

"Hey, yeah, good memory, girl," Hank said.

After a half hour in the air, she said, "Will you tell me when we are over Nevada?"

"We're going to land in Nevada, in Reno. But we don't have to change planes. Passengers get off, and new ones get on, and then we fly to Elko."

"We're not stopping in Winnemucca, are we?" Sunny asked.

"No, honey. We fly over Winnemucca," Hank told her. "Why? Were you ever there?"

"I think we lived in a trailer park in that town. I didn't like it," she whispered.

"Sunny," Hank began slowly, "did you call the operator and say you thought you were with the wrong mommy?"

"Yes. From Winnemucca," she answered.

"I … I wish I'd known," Hank said. Could he ever tell her the FBI scoured that town looking for the telephone with the numbers one, six, and two?

The afternoon thermals created some turbulence over the Sierras, and Sunny clutched Hank and Susan's hands. They didn't let go until they landed in Reno, and then Hank went to find somebody to check on Paraíso. Susan and Sunny ate sandwiches provided by the airline service and watched people board the plane for the second flight.

After Hank came back and assured them the dog was fine, Sunny said, "This is so strange. I could get up right now and go talk to anyone I wanted to. If there was an empty set, I could sit down and have a normal conversation. I wouldn't have to worry about what I said or about getting punished later for breaking the rules. You can't imagine what that feels like, that freedom."

When they were in the air once more, with the whole of Nevada, sparse, clean, and inviting below them, she had to close her eyes for a moment. "You just can't imagine," she said again.

They touched down in Elko forty-five minutes later and encouraged Sunny to buy some Indian jewelry in the small gift shop inside the airport. "Should I choose things for everyone at home?" she asked.

"Sunny, you are going to be the greatest gift they'll ever have," her father said.

Dancing Horse had left the truck in the parking lot and gotten a ride back to the ranch with one of his cousins from the Res that night he had rushed the Roses to the airport to get to Sunny. Now, Hank and Susan and their long-missing daughter headed toward the truck with Paraíso practically prancing beside them. It was still daylight, but huge summer cumulus clouds cast giant shadows on the ground. The shepherd leaped over each dark edge and tugged on his leash.

Sunny looked up. "This sky is bluer than any sky I remember. Is it always like this?" she asked.

"In the summer," Hank answered.

"Oh, I knew I loved Nevada!" she cried.

They had about seventy-five miles to go. Sunny said she didn't remember any of it, but as the sun went down, she pressed her face to the window facing west and called out the colors—scarlet, bruised purple, sunflower gold, lady-slipper pink, thunderstorm gray, hematite black. And the first day of her new life was almost over.

◀◀◆▶▶

When they drove under the sign at the ranch, Sunny happily translated—"Ranch of the Blue Sky." Hank could see she didn't recognize the trees, the junipers had grown so tall, or the siding on the new hay barn, or the pond he had put in two years ago. Even the inside of the main house was different. One wall had been knocked out of some guest quarters to expand the living area. The first thing she recognized was her room. Susan and Hank had not changed it in eight years. They apologized for its small, child-decorated atmosphere and explained that when they learned she was alive, they could only think of seeing her. They didn't think that the room she would come home to might not suit her.

The twelve-year-old picked up some dolls she used to love, running her hands through their silky, blonde hair and feeling the starched petticoats and porcelain skin. She placed Grey Boy back at the top of her pile of stuffed animals.

"I remember this … but can I fix it for who I am now?"

"Of course," Susan said.

Then Sunny sat down on the narrow bed with its ruffled pink bedspread with colorful pink and purple ponies prancing about on the soft cloth. "But who am I?" she asked.

"You can be whoever you want to be," Hank said.

"Did you think I was coming back?" she asked. She curled up a little as if a creature hunkering down in its shell.

"It's what we lived for," Susan answered.

"Hey, a few of the wranglers want to see you," Hank said to open her up. "Do you remember Billy and Tyrone?"

"Oh yes!"

"And Angie?"

"I … think so."

"Dancing Horse, Willow, and their daughter, Rachel?" Susan asked.

"Rachel Endless Rain! Yes! Do I get to see them all at once?"

"Rachel's teaching at Harvard. She'll be home at Christmas. But the others are coming over after dinner. There are some new hands, but we only asked the ones you knew for tonight," Susan explained.

"May I sleep until dinner?"

"Of course, darling," Hank said. He set her few books and clothes that she had kept on the plush carpet.

"Did I really like this *pink*?" she asked.

"You did. And the purple too. What would you like now?" Susan asked.

"Yellow … to go with my real name. Oh, Momma, I feel so safe now. I'm glad you stayed the same, even though I changed so much.

Susan opened her arms to her almost-a-stranger child.

"Um, no … no hugs." Sunny kept her eyes on the pink carpet.

"That's okay, Sunny. We won't always do or say the right things. Don't be afraid to tell us," her mother said.

"One time Mommy—I have to call her that still, you know—Mommy said I was a lot of trouble, but she was keeping me because she was *exacting revenge*. Do you know what she meant?"

"I'm afraid I do," Hank said. He was so avoiding this conversation.

"First tell me if you know what her real name is."

Hank hesitated. If he kept the truth from her now, he could ruin the trust she was just gaining in him.

"Why can't I know it?" she persisted.

"You can. It's Liana."

"Do you know her?"

"Believe it or not, I met her when I was the age you are now."

"Really? Did she hurt you?"

"Yes, Sunny, she did, but I guess it wasn't enough. I thought I'd never see her again. I didn't even tell your mother until recently. You should never keep secrets from the ones you love."

"What did she do to you, Daddy?"

Susan discreetly left the room. Hank figured she knew enough, even though she had never let him tell her the details. He knew that conversation would be harder than this one if it ever came.

"She was five years older. I was a child. She molested me."

Sunny gasped. "Oh, Daddy, if I'd known that, I would've killed her!"

"That's what your mother said. That's what *my* mother said, the woman whose name you share. Serena."

"Why wasn't Liana locked up then?"

"She disappeared."

"She's good at that," Sunny said, and then, looking away from him, she added, "I think she … did that to me too. But I can't talk about it."

112

"It's okay, Sunny. We all have things we can't talk about."

"The doctors want me to, but it's all mixed up in my mind with growing up, being clean, being trapped, being helpless. When I try to say the actual words, my throat won't let me. Do you think the investigators will ask me again?"

"I don't know, Sunny. What do you think will happen if you … tell more than you have?"

"They probably won't let me tell just a little, and I don't know how to draw the line between what I hated and what I liked."

"Exactly," Hank said.

She looked across the room at one of her great-grandmother's watercolors, still not meeting her father's eyes. Framed in rough white pine was the image of a group of children on different-sized horses with the tall figure of her great-grandfather Henry in the center.

"That's a new thing I want to do!" Sunny exclaimed.

"What's that?"

"I want to paint!"

"I'll give you all of my grandmother Helen's supplies, brushes and paper and sketching pencils. Some stuff isn't good anymore, like white-out and paint. I should have thrown it away, but her hands touched those things. One of her pictures saved my father's life."

"How could a painting do that?" Sunny asked.

"It was given to a woman that tried to kill him and your grandmother Serena. That woman agreed to take her meds and not be any more trouble to my folks if she could have that picture," Hank said.

"But what's so special about that painting?"

"Well, first of all, it was my dad's favorite, so the woman still felt connected to him or maybe even that she had some control over him. And second, the things in the picture had a deep and healing meaning for all those involved."

"What happened to it?"

Hank hesitated for just a moment. He couldn't look in her eyes when he answered. "Liana stole it and sold it. But my dad found it at an auction years later and brought it back home. It's over the fireplace in the living room."

"Oh, I can't wait to see it! And just think, Daddy, even with two bad women, the painting and I survived."

"Yes, you did!"

"Maybe they'll have some paints at school."

"I'll get you some. School's about two months away," he said.

"Daddy? Am I twelve?"

"Yes, you are."

Sunny got up off the bed and searched the room until she found just what she wanted. She methodically pulled some buttons from some old clothes, of course too small for her now, and lined up twelve of them in a neat row on the top of the dresser.

10

◀◀◀◆▶▶▶

The summer of Sunny's twelfth year was a turning point for everyone. All the things Sunny couldn't say she put down on paper with paint and charcoal. There were splendid replications of the Sierra Nevada's in snow; stark, leafless aspens scattered amongst the green pines; California redwoods towering over faint trails winding into the mist; turquoise and emerald waves crashing on a Pacific, bleached-white beach; a red horse rearing out of the foam. But most disturbing was a black and white sketch of an old, claw-foot bathtub with items lying on a tile floor and around the faucets: a plastic-handled hairbrush; a stack of washcloths, dirty ones mixed with clean; a child's dress and underwear heaped in a pile; and one strand of water-colored bright-red hair draped over one side of the tub. Another revealed a wreck of a house trailer with snow falling heavily around the shapeless structure, that same piece of red hair caught in a crack on the porch railing.

She spoke freely with these images. But one could only guess what had taken place in these locations, secrets and lies in the shadows. Even the pretty ones cried, *Help, don't you see me. I'm right here. I can't get out of this by myself.* When Hank studied these paintings and drawings, he knew she was speaking for him too. Some of the abuse he suffered at the hands of Liana, no one knew, even his long-buried mother and father and certainly not his wife. He had told everybody he loved that woman while she was tantalizing him, putting moves on his head and his body in ways he didn't really understand.

And then there were the posters, which neither Hank nor Susan knew what to make of. At first, the words were simple enough: *no toast* and *put dog's kibble outside*. In a while, they became more strange and troubling: *don't cover windows … can't use Ivory soap … afraid of long-handled spoons*. By her great-grandmother's painting of the abused bronc in the round pen—*I know how he feels*. The wranglers not only didn't touch her, they didn't touch each other in her presence. Hank told them to wait for her to understand that touching wasn't always bad.

One day in an August rainstorm, Hank and Sunny brushed horses in the barn. His daughter was quiet, but when she started on the fourth horse, she suddenly put the grooming tool down and turned to her father. "I can't do this," she said.

"Why, darling?" her dad asked, going over to where she stood by her grandmother Serena's seventeen-year-old Akhal-Teke mare.

"Because she likes it. The horse craves that soft touching, that … rubbing. The more she likes it, the more I don't want to do it," Sunny said.

"Isn't it all right if the horse likes it?"

"I don't know," she said, and then her voice got very soft. "I hated it. It scared me. It can be a bad thing."

The mare side-stepped closer to Sunny. Her shoulder brushed Sunny's arm.

"See? She's asking for it," Sunny declared.

"Here's the difference if I understand you right, sweetheart," Hank began. "She's asking for it, but you don't have to give it. You have a choice in the matter. You have a voice. You can make her stop leaning on you. You can put the curry comb away and clean saddles instead. But listen, it's never bad if you both want the same thing and give it out of love."

"Ah."

"Make a choice, Sunny. Do it right now," Hank told her.

She put her arms round the horse's neck. The mare shuddered

with pleasure. Sunny let herself feel the touch of the horse, and then she asked, "Was Grandma Serena killed on this horse?"

"We're not sure. My folks were both struck by lightning, but the mare made it home. Serena didn't," Hank said.

"I'm sorry, Daddy. About your mom. I'm really trying to figure out feelings that don't have anything to do with the horse," she said.

"Yes. I know."

A week or two after that conversation, Hank hired a senior boy, a Native American called Thomas Heart-of-the-Hawk, the son of a former track-running mate of his, to tutor Sunny in the subjects she might have missed in her haphazard education. Hank thought she might be wary of an older girl. His daughter would be skipping the sixth grade. The boy's sister was in the seventh grade and would introduce Sunny to some of her friends.

The two became close immediately. Thomas made friends with Paraíso and gave Sunny a few Native American herbs to treat the dog's arthritis. Tom spoke Spanish, as well as his Sioux tongue, and the two young people packed their conversations with three languages. The only unusual thing about Thomas was that he was Catholic.

Hank said to Susan, "I think it's okay that Thomas goes to St. Mary's, don't you?"

"It's okay as long as he doesn't take her away from her Iroquois traditions. They're probably at least as old as the Catholic Church," she answered.

The boy promised not to talk about his faith, but it wouldn't have mattered. Sunny met St. Mary's new priest at a get-acquainted youth function that summer. He was a young, black South African from Soweto on an exchange program where priests were sent to areas that the Church decided needed special service. It was no coincidence St. Mary's was located near the Reservation. Susan and Hank had introduced themselves to the African, Father Azenwa, at a pow-wow. He danced with the Natives, his black robes swirling, his handsome, dark face seeming like one of the brown-skinned warriors of their local tribes. He did not speak of rituals or sacraments. He learned the Native American prayers. He remembered peoples' Indian names. The Roses had thought about going to St. Mary's but were so consumed with finding Sunny or with finding a life without Sunny that they stayed away from this beautiful, charismatic man and his fundamental Church.

Now, their daughter seemed as anxious to be in the cathedral as she was about starting school. She read the Bible daily with as much passion as she showed learning to ride again. Hank bought her a flashy Arabian mare from a highly respected local breeder when the eighteen-year-old Grey Boy could not keep up with her teenage demands. But when Hank noticed the dish-faced, arched-neck, gorgeous equine pacing in her private, extra-large paddock, unridden several days a week, he had to ask his daughter why she had stopped doing things with her horse.

"Oh, I love her," Sunny said, "but listen to this. I can't stop reading these scriptures. They redeem my whole life." And she quoted long verses, mostly from the New Testament, her cheeks red, her eyes bright, as if she had stepped into a new world, which perhaps she had. "'Now for a little while you may have had to suffer grief in all kinds of trials. These have come to you so that your faith—of greater worth than gold, which perishes even though refined by fire—may be proved genuine and may result in praise, glory, and honor when Jesus Christ is revealed.'" She looked at Hank as if that explained her absence from the barn.

When Sunny finally mounted her mare one Sunday after church and went across the diagonal of the outdoor arena doing flying changes, Hank stood by the rail and felt his heart leap. Sunny, with her dark hair, pale brown skin, and almond eyes, looked like a princess from a faraway land. She merged with the horse, as Hank's mother had done, in such a natural way, her seat bones solid on the mare's back like a full-blooded Indian, her hair bouncing as the horse changed leads, and her hands barely moving on the reins as she circled and half-passed her way around the ring. She halted Grey Girl effortlessly where her father was leaning on the top rail.

"Nice job, darling. Doesn't that make you happy?" he said.

She said, "Daddy, did you know there are a lot of horses in the Bible? Especially in Revelation?"

"I guess I didn't. What do you think it means?" he asked her.

"It means I'll be able to ride forever!" she said.

Susan created a tasseled, gold and purple brocade costume for the fair specialty class. Hank watched his daughter practice with gold slippers on her feet and purple robes rippling over the grey back against the arched tail of the Arab, but he supposed she wouldn't go.

The day of the fair, a few weeks after she entered seventh grade, she went to St. Mary's in the morning and did not return for her costume or her horse. They found one of her posters tacked to Grey Girl's stall door—*I have gone to catechism class.* She came home wearing a slim gold chain with a tiny cross. She said, "I couldn't go to the fair. I hope I don't need a poster to tell you why."

"I'm glad the Church gives you comfort," her mother said.

"It's more than that," their daughter said. "It gives me purpose."

"What purpose would that be?" Susan asked.

"To learn how I can serve God," she said.

"There are many ways to serve God without being in the Catholic Church," Susan said.

"It's a choice, Momma. A choice to be good. Maybe someday I can explain it to you."

"Don't wait too long," Susan said, but Sunny was already through the door into her room.

"She probably has homework. I wouldn't worry," Hank said. "We have to accept that some of her choices are not going to be ours."

Then Father Azenwa showed up one evening, apologizing if they hadn't expected him. "Sunny wanted me to visit with you someplace other than the church where I don't see you too often."

Sunny burst into the room. "Oh, Mom, Dad, I forgot to put up a poster about Father coming!"

"Well, it's okay," Susan said. "We'd enjoy Father Azenwa's company."

They sat in the living room with the fire sending its friendly warmth into the air. Luz was fixing tea for everyone, and they talked about the weather, Sunny's classes at school, the youth group at church, and Hank's talented horses—all safe subjects, Hank thought.

"I should like to see Sunny ride one of these days," the priest said.

"She has a wonderful mare, an Arab. They look like champions together to me," Hank said. "I hoped she would grab her passion for horses and hang on for dear life. It seems more grounded than a spiritual life."

Father Azenwa went on unfazed, "Sunny told me one of the first things she recognized after years with the kidnapper was a grey horse grazing in a pasture in California."

So it was out, more of the missing years, the experiences the Roses thought they would never hear. But it was still safe territory. Hank wondered what else she might have told the priest. Of course, he could not repeat it. Sunny went to help Luz in the kitchen.

"Are you bothered that Sunny has chosen the Catholic faith?" he asked suddenly.

Man, this guy doesn't pull any punches, Hank thought.

"Only if she's being coerced in any way," Susan said.

She can dish it out too. Hank smiled.

"I would never do that, Mrs. Rose," the priest said. "Sunny came to the cathedral with Thomas. She told me the first time that she felt as if she belonged. She wanted the sacraments. But she was not qualified yet."

"You have to qualify for God's love?" Hank asked.

"Perhaps I misstated," Father said. "The journey toward the sacraments is a … learning period. God's love is always there."

Sunny sat down with them again. "I like the learning part," she said. "I was denied so much, you can't imagine."

"We want to imagine, Sunny," Susan said quietly. "But you are taking another journey without *us.* Do you know how hard that is?"

"But you can come with me!" their daughter said. "We can share all the secrets of the Church, the only way to find God."

"We would just as soon know *your* secrets," Hank said.

"I have encouraged her to tell you everything," Father Azenwa said, "but just to be clear, she hasn't even told me. The Church is there to support her, no matter what."

"We appreciate your candor, Father, but my husband and I find the dogma of most churches very limiting," Susan said.

"For me, it has opened up the whole world," the priest said and gave them an expansive smile.

Luz brought the tea in with a plate of cookies she had made from one of Marta's recipes. No one spoke for a few minutes. Hank liked the priest. He felt Susan was being a bit confrontational. He thought *We may never have his convictions ... or his peace.*

"My father's cook and one of his dearest friends was a Catholic from Tanzania," Hank said.

"Oh my, what a small world! I should like to know him. Is he still in this country?"

"He's buried next to my parents about five miles from here."

Sunny dropped her cup of tea into the saucer, breaking both pieces. Tea ran onto her lap and then the carpet.

"Oh, Daddy! I just remembered someone. Jason! Uncle Jason!"

"He's buried up there too, sweetie. We didn't want to shock you with that news when you first came home, and then it seemed you'd forgotten him," Hank said gently.

"He read to me and helped me with Grey Boy. He loved me."

"Yes ... after you ... were taken, his health deteriorated. He spent two nights searching the fairgrounds—every corner, every place a child might hide or be trapped. He was not a young man. Waiting for you ... well, he just couldn't do it."

"Oh, I'm so sorry," Sunny said. "I was so young. I probably wasn't very respectful. And then I left him."

"Sunny, you don't need to be sorry for anything. You were four years old. You had no control over what happened," Hank said, trying to console her.

"But don't you see? That's why I have to have control over what I do now."

"We do see that, sweetheart. We'll trust Father Azenwa to guide you, but please don't shut us out," Susan said.

"I can't let you in until I understand completely what happened to me. I love this place, my horses, Paraíso. I love you. But I think my heart belongs to God," the girl said, those honest words falling on their ears for the first time.

"Mr. and Mrs. Rose, I hope I haven't added to your concerns over those lost years with Sunny. I'll do everything to keep you in the circle of her choices. I'll not influence her, just listen to her."

"Father Azenwa, that's all we could ask. Really, we're grateful for your presence in her life," Hank said, and then asked more boldly, "But doesn't she seem to be in a hurry? Shouldn't this process take some time?"

"Well, you're right, Mr. Rose. Usually becoming a Catholic when the child wasn't born into the faith can take months. But, you see, the bishop will be here at Christmas. He only comes to this far outpost of Catholicism once a year or so. He is the one who presides over the confirmation. I think in Sunny's case, her desires should be considered. She has begun her catechism classes. She'll be baptized next week. I hope you'll attend."

"Of course, Father. We want to be a part of Sunny's life, wherever that takes her," Hank promised.

"I knew you'd understand," he said. "I'll leave you then. I have a big day ahead. I'll look forward to seeing you again. Peace and grace on your household." He made the sign of the cross.

Hank gripped the priest's hand. "My mother and father were given that blessing the night before they were married. It means a lot to me. Thank you."

"I'll walk Father out," Sunny offered.

Hank gathered a stunned Susan into his arms and said, "I think it's going to be all right."

"Oh, Henry, it's not what I pictured for our daughter."

"What you pictured is what she'd be like if she hadn't been gone for eight years."

"You're right. You're absolutely right. I have to start seeing things through your eyes. You're so much steadier than I am when times get rough."

"I wonder where I got that from," Hank said, remembering hearing of the balanced demeanor of his mother facing a mad woman with a gun out in the desert. "Anyway, I think we have to start seeing things through Sunny's eyes."

Sunny raced back in. "What do you think? Isn't he great?"

"He's a wonderful man, Sunny," Hank answered. "Your mother and I aren't so sure about the Church."

"Why?"

"I don't understand what's there for you," Susan said.

"Answers. I need answers. The Church has answers."

"Maybe the answers are in your own heart," her mother said.

"Oh, I wish that were true! It would be so much easier then. I could hold my head up and say, 'Here I am. Accept me or not. I am Serena Sun Rose, kidnap victim, fool to follow her captor everywhere and sometimes even *like* her!' In a few weeks, I can say, 'I am Sunny Rose, Catholic! It gives a huge dimension to my life, a *conversion* to something much grander than my spare being.'"

"How did you learn such adult words?" Susan asked.

"I always got an A in vocabulary," she answered. "I can say all those words in Spanish too!"

"Why don't you aim for some university degree and become a translator for the UN or something," Hank suggested.

"Because there's no place for God there or for what he wants me to do."

"What if there is no God, the kind of God who has plans for his creations?" Susan dared to ask.

"Oh, Momma, if there were no God, I might still be with … Mommy."

"God didn't open Liana's car door," Hank said, a bit determined to win this argument.

But Sunny was ready. "The Bible says, *hope does not disappoint us, because God has poured out his love into our hearts by the Holy Spirit.* I had *hope* burning up in that car. It was the only thing I had. And just enough breath to scream. I was not disappointed. God did open that car!"

"Well, if he did, then I am truly grateful," Hank said.

"Me too," Susan added. "We'll honor your faith, Serena Sun."

She kissed them good night, a first. She seemed so happy. How could they take that away from her with their grown-up logic, their experience of the world that she had never had? She was still a child, grasping at the shiny baubles of hope and love and good men like Father Azenwa, not believing that there *were* disappointments, there were tragedies that could strike like lightning out of a clear blue sky.

◀◀◀◆▶▶▶

After Sunny settled into the routine of seventh grade, she opened up more to the parents she had stopped believing in when she was five, a mother and a father who listened to her, did not hit her, did not even knock on the bathroom door. She had even quit locking it.

"You can't imagine how wonderful it is to be called by my own name!" she said one day as they all sat at the dinner table waiting for Luz's taco pie with tomatoes and cilantro from the garden. "I can have an opinion. I can read whatever I want. I can like whoever I want."

After she organized a riding club and insisted they include Native Americans, especially horsemen and women from the Reservation, she seemed to gain a following. She seldom came home alone after school. There were always two or three classmates with her. They played games on horseback or studied in the kitchen, sometimes helping Luz or Susan with dinner and staying for dinner. Hank often had to drive kids home after ten o'clock in the evening.

One night, she waited up for him. "Can I tell you something, Daddy?"

"Sure, sweetheart," he said. His breath quickened, because so many things had not been said yet.

"I've had to tell everyone that I don't like to be hugged. It makes me feel funny. Do you think I should say that I'm seeing a doctor about it to find out why, other than the obvious?"

"Sunny, I think you should tell people whatever you're comfortable with," he said.

"Well, I can't wear a poster! I could say something like, 'Hug me later after I've seen my psychiatrist'!"

"I'm glad to see you haven't lost your sense of humor," Hank said.

"Did I ever have one?" she asked.

"Girl, you wouldn't believe the stuff you pulled on your uncle Jason! One day you got on Grey Boy before Jason got out to the arena. You were sitting backward in the saddle with a straight face. I don't know how you did it. 'I'm ready, Jase,' you said. 'Which way do you want to me to circle first?' Of course, he played along."

"What'd he do?"

"'Let's start with figure eights,' he said. And you said, 'Do I look okay, Jase?' 'Look fine to me,' he said. 'Kick that Boy now. Maybe we'll try some jumps today.' That cracked you both up. You just about fell off that horse!"

"Thanks, Dad. Thanks for showing me I was a real person."

"Honey, even when you were gone, you were still a real person to us."

"But I wasn't. I was a ghost of the real Sunny, a Baby, a Rainbow. Mr. Bowen was the first person who really saw me, and there was nothing he could do."

"He gave you books. He listened when you spoke. I thank God for him, and as you know, that is not my way."

"I thank God for him too," she said.

Before that week was out, Sunny had joined the drama club and tried out for the Junior Varsity Football cheerleading team. Because of her persistence and talent, she and another Native American girl were chosen.

Hearing Sunny talk about this flurry of activities, Hank was reminded of the way he was liked and respected after Henry Dancing Horse became his friend and mentor when Hank was only six years old. He thought how people sometimes feared what they didn't know, people of different colors and religions, but when they realized how rich and meaningful these seemingly dissonant friendships could be, then they wanted that for themselves and opened up. At least he hoped that was true.

It seemed that school was going extremely well for his daughter, but the big questions about Sunny's abuse and about the Catholic

Church remained. And strangely, he thought, the two seemed connected. One day she came home visibly shaken. She had seen both the psychiatrist and the priest that afternoon. It was late. Hank was tired from rounding cows and calves onto the winter range closer to the ranch where hay could be rolled out to them. He was relaxing in his father's old, easy chair when Sunny startled him.

"Dad, you have to tell me what Liana did to you," she said.

"Oh, Sunny, it was a lifetime ago. I put all that behind me," he said.

"Well, it's not behind me. I need to know."

"Why?"

"Dr. Dan said it would help me figure out some things."

Hank noticed she called her psychiatrist by his first name, but that was probably nothing compared to what else she might be pronouncing for that man's ears alone.

"Sunny, what she did to me was, at that time, more than a boy of twelve could say no to. I hate to admit it, but I enjoyed her attention. I don't imagine you enjoyed anything that woman did to you."

"But what if *she* enjoyed it, and I let her. I didn't fight back. I wanted to please her!" Sunny said.

"Darling, Liana said she loved me. What she did to you was because she hated me. It's not the same."

"But what she did to me, was it mental abuse, or was it … sexual?"

"What do you think?"

"I think it was both."

"And what would you do if you knew?"

"I'd have something to tell Father in my first confession," she answered. She was fidgeting a little.

Hank reached over and took her hand. She was sitting across from him on the ottoman. She didn't shrink back as she had earlier in the year.

"My dear child," Hank began, "you have nothing to confess. The priest should hear Liana's confession."

"But it's mine that will get me to my first communion," she told him.

"And why is that so important to you?"

"Because it's the only way to reach the flame of the Holy Spirit."

"By confessing to something you had no control over?"

"I had more control than you think, Dad. I *used* Liana to get what I wanted—books and school and camping on the beach instead of staying in a motel," she answered.

"You used her to be safe. There's no law against that."

"Are you sure? What about God's law? There're plenty of those I broke. I can only fix my sin by being a Catholic."

"I'll tell you what you want to know, Sunny, but I'll thank you not to repeat *my* sin to Father Azenwa."

So he told his daughter about his affair with Liana, the five-year catastrophe that led to violence and ultimately the kidnapping. He didn't spare her any details. Maybe it would shock her into understanding how at fault Liana was. Or maybe it would set her back in her recovery. It was a chance he had to take. He told her how at first Liana teased him, then demanded physical proof of his attraction to her, then threatened him when he didn't do what she wanted, then killed two of his dogs, one of them the grandmother of Sunny's own Paraíso, and stole his own grandmother Helen's painting.

"That's it! That's it! My confirmation name. It'll be Marta *Helen!*" she exclaimed, seeming to be lost in a world other than the one he was revealing. But suddenly she came back into his shattered past.

"Dad, I can't tell you what Liana did to me, but I can tell you what it was like." She closed her eyes for a moment, envisioning. "It was like dancing in red snow."

Hank sat straight up. "What did you say?"

"You know, that red hair falling all around me, touching me, her fingers like ice, her arms smothering me, dancing in red snow."

He released her hand with a gentle squeeze. "Honey, I'm really beat tonight. Can we talk more later?"

"Sure, Daddy. I could never tell Mom this stuff." She bolted out of the room.

Hank closed his eyes, and the words appeared in his reluctant memory, fragments of his mother's poem about Carla—*I have danced in the red snow / where she finds me open … I do not flee with my fresh wounds … I feel her hunger / chance that dangerous ground for a little death … I put my paws in her traps … Those traces of crimson / floating the white tide? It's only my heart /unconsumed.*

I know about that, Hank thought. But how prophetic those sensual words for the woman his mother had loved and couldn't stay with. Sunny could not have seen those words on those scraps of notepaper he had saved, and yet they flowed from her lips as if born there.

Susan came into the room just then and said, "Henry, let's go to bed."

Later, he held his Iroquois wife so far removed from the sins of father and daughter, not even believing in such things. His heart wept making love to Susan for the irreversible damage Liana had done to his family, for his sin of having desired the abductor himself, then rejecting her and sending her down that terrible path.

11

◀◀◀◆▶▶▶

S now fell before Thanksgiving, painting the carmine bluffs,
pink shale arroyos, and dusky desert floor a fearsome white.
No trails could be discerned or ranch roads followed without
markers. Hank looked out from the comfort of the log-fire heated
house and felt the change deeply. Where were the markers for Sunny?
She wore a gold cross, she knelt at an altar foreign to him, she believed
the priest changed the bread and the wine into flesh and blood, and
she sometimes still put posters up for Susan and him to read. The
last one said—*Christ is the Way.*

When she came home from her first confession, Hank asked,
"Can you tell me what you said?"

"Absolutely not," she answered. She picked up a blank poster and
went to her room.

A few days later, the sign was tacked to her bedroom door. It
read—*I am not yet found.*

Hank took that one down before her mother could see it.

Luz and Susan decorated the rooms with colored lights, a couple
of small pines that Hank hated cutting down, ornaments from as far
back as Henry and Helen Rose, fake snow with pieces of cinnamon
stacked like fences, little horse statues balanced behind in the white
fluff, and glass icicles hanging everyplace.

"Isn't there enough of some of that stuff *outside*?" Hank teased.

Just before Christmas, the Roses and a few of the wranglers went to St. Mary's for Sunny's confirmation. Hank felt the solemnity of the occasion but could not know what was in his daughter's heart. Susan asked him not to sit too close to the front. Eleven young people stood before Father Azenwa and a bishop from California. They affirmed their beliefs, asked the help of the Holy Spirit, and knelt on a rail at the appropriate times. Sunny was beyond radiant in Serena's wedding dress that had been her great-grandmother Helen's wedding dress, her oh so black hair falling down the back of the white satin in glossy waves. She stated her name in a clear voice as *Marta Helen* as she had told her father she would do. Susan gave a small gasp of surprise.

Father Azenwa shook everyone's hand, and some teens from the youth group served refreshments. The Roses held back a little. Most of the parents were Catholic and knew so much more about what had just taken place. Hank recognized folks that had been guests at the ranch or attended clinics there. Some of them tried to draw Hank and Susan into conversations, but Hank wished those people could just understand that when your child has been abducted and abused for eight years, you aren't the same as other parents. Part of *you* has been abducted, a part you will never get back.

Sunny found her way to them in the crowd.

"It was a beautiful service, sweetheart," Hank said, hugging her briefly.

Susan smoothed some hair back from her daughter's shining face.

"I feel reborn," Sunny said.

The priest thanked them for coming and invited them to Christmas Mass. Hank really liked the man but knew that Susan would never spend her Christmas day in a Catholic church.

She said immediately, "That is kind of you, Father, but we have our own traditions. Sunny can attend if she wishes. Your traditions seem to be healing her."

"I believe the love of her family is healing her," he said.

"We can hope, Father," Hank said.

On the way home, Sunny jabbered on like the four-year-old they had lost. "Maybe I can go to the fair next year. I just feel like God would never let anything bad happen to me," she finally announced.

Hank thought at once, *He let it happen more than eight years ago! What's different about God now?* But he knew the answer. God wasn't different; Sunny was. It continued to worry Hank that Sunny could not talk about what had been done to her. Her summer posters had been glaring hints of some kind of torture. And the FBI insisted they needed more details to lock Liana up forever, if not execute her.

Then he had another disturbing thought. *If one believed in God, one would have to forgive! Would this newly-embraced Church ultimately ask Sunny to do that?* He knew his own father had forgiven the woman who had harassed him and even killed two of his best horses. And Julian was definitely not Catholic. Hank decided you didn't have to believe in God to do the right thing. But he didn't know if forgiving was the right thing anyway.

Sunny, sitting between Hank and Susan in the car, said, "I belong to God now."

Her mother asked, "When did you think you didn't belong to God?"

"When I was in Liana's arms," she replied instantly.

Hank let that one go.

But later that day, Sunny said to her father privately, "I almost have her out of me," and Hank felt sure Liana would be forgotten and unforgiven, a small token of the justice that was her due.

◄◄◄◆►►►

In March, in a snowstorm, Sunny raced into the house from outside, crying, "Mom! Dad! The purple crocus is coming up. It's too early! They'll never make it!"

"They always make it, darling," Hank said. "You just don't remember."

"Do you think I'll make it?"

"I do," he said.

"I missed a lot, didn't I?" she said.

"Mostly we old folks moping around for their bright Sunny," he answered.

"I wasn't very *bright* all those years."

"But were there bright spots? Can you tell me some more of those, like the time you rode the horse into the ocean? Things like that?"

"I can try. Oh, here's one, although I don't know if you'll like it," she said.

"I'll like anything that made you happy," he said.

"Okay. Well, there was a priest at the mission school Mommy sent me to. He listened to me. He gave me little presents when I memorized Bible verses or said a good prayer."

"He didn't …"

"Oh, no, no, no. He was a wonderful man. He gave me pretty rocks he found or flowers he had dried and pressed in between his favorite verses. He walked me to class and told me about the Indians that used to live and work at the mission. I didn't know I was a Native American, but I think he suspected it. Then he'd see me with Mommy. Sometimes she didn't wear her wig and just let that red hair fall all around her face. He couldn't figure me out after that, but he made me feel real."

"A bright spot in the same sentence as *Mommy*. I think that's good, Sunny," Hank said.

"Like the crocus in the snow," she said.

"Just like that," he said.

The phone rang. Susan picked it up and called to Sunny, "It's for you! It's a *boy*."

Sunny talked for quite a while and then came out to the living room where Hank was building up the fire, and Susan was reading.

"It was Thomas Heart-of-the-Hawk," she said. She sat down next to her mother. "He asked me to go to the senior prom with him."

"I don't think so," Hank said. "You are a mature young lady, but you are not quite thirteen. Thomas is what, seventeen?"

"Eighteen," Sunny said.

"I know you got along fine when he was tutoring you, but how well do you know him?" Hank asked.

"We see each other a lot at church. Sometime we lead the Bible classes. I like Thomas, but I don't think I want to go to the prom. I don't want to hurt his feelings or have him think I'm uncomfortable with him because of his race."

"You're half Iroquois," Susan said. "Why would he think you're a racist?"

"I don't live like many Native Americans have to. I don't want for a thing. I have *white* relatives."

"Call him and see what he says," Hank advised. "It's always better to go with the truth."

"Well, I don't know about that," Sunny said. "My lies might have kept me alive."

"That was different," Susan told her.

"Do you guys think I'm lying to you because I won't tell you exactly what happened with Liana?"

"No," they both said at the same time.

And then Hank added, "If I asked you a direct question about Liana's abuse, you'd tell me, wouldn't you?"

"Yes," she answered just as quickly. "But don't do it yet." She picked up her dad's cell phone and went to her room.

She was back a while later with a perplexed look on her face.

"What'd he say?" Hank asked.

"He said he wouldn't go with anyone else. He'd rather just come over for dinner and talk, if that's okay with you."

"Oh, that would be nice, Sunny. What a thoughtful young man," Susan said.

"Why do you say that, Mom?"

"He's trying not to hurt *your* feelings. He's making it about spending time with you as a friend if he can't be your date," she answered.

"I guess I have a lot to learn, don't I?"

"We all do, my darling daughter," Hank said.

The prom was still two months away. When Sunny wasn't at school or church, she helped with the new calves, blanketing of horses, cleaning tack, and organizing the garden for spring planting. She didn't put up any posters during that time. She bloomed like the hardy crocus in their cold beds. Hank counted each of those days as canceling ones he had missed. Susan fixed her hair, and when her daughter was doing homework, she leaned over her at her desk whenever Sunny would let her.

Hank saw that Sunny was more reticent with her mother and rarely asked her personal questions or sought her attention. Was it because the kidnapper was a woman and now all women were threats to her stability? If a man had taken her, would Sunny be more shy around him? *Does abuse really have a gender?* he asked himself. Or was it simply that Sunny and he were both molested by the same person and shared some kind of grief over it, some kind of *understanding* that Susan never could, so their daughter felt more of a bond with him?

Most of the friends Sunny brought home were boys. Hank could not think of the name of one of her girlfriends. One Saturday, he decided to ask her about it. He went out to help her in the garden. She was thinning seedlings so the strongest plants could survive. He got down on his hands and knees next to her in a row of onions.

"Can I ask you something, sweetheart?" he said.

"You can ask. I may not answer."

"Do you have any … girlfriends?"

She stiffened. "What do you mean?"

"Maybe I didn't say it right. I just don't see you doing things with girls or mentioning a girl's name now and then, like someone who was a good friend."

"I *know* girls, of course. I teach girls at Sunday school. I help a couple of sixth grade girls with math. But some girls act afraid of me." She pulled up a few more baby onions. "One time I got close to a ninth grader—Belinda James. She's Catholic. She's smart. I could tell her about my horses, ranch life, you know. Sometimes we'd discuss books and poetry and my Iroquois heritage. She didn't treat me like an untouchable."

Sunny sat back and looked up at the blue Nevada sky. She said, "But that was the problem. She started asking me things like 'Have you ever kissed a girl?' and 'Will you still be my friend if I hold hands with Mara at camp?' I told her I'd still like her but probably not want to *see* that relationship or talk about it. She quit coming to Bible study and would barely speak to me passing in the halls at school."

"Do you think there's something wrong with being gay?" Hank asked.

"No. But apparently Belinda thought that I had a problem with it and didn't want anything more to do with me. I don't *fit* with girls. I can't explain myself to them." She dug her hands angrily into the rich soil.

"Honey, wait! Don't pull up so many."

"Oh, I don't care," she said. "I'm only doing this so I won't have to think about things like why I don't fit!" She got up and stalked toward the house.

Hank carefully replanted a few tiny onions that Sunny had plucked out in such haste. He decided he should not have asked his daughter those questions so early in her recovery, but he did now have a hint of an answer to his own question. *Sunny doesn't think she fits with her own mother,* he thought as he trudged back to the house.

◄◄◄◆►►►

The night of the prom, Thomas showed up at the door with a beautiful corsage for Sunny. "You deserve flowers anyway, even if I can't dance with you," he said.

"That's so sweet! I'll keep them in a special place," Sunny said.

Luz had cooked an African meal she had learned from Askay. They sat at the dining room table to give some formality to the occasion, and Luz announced the courses of the meal in the African tradition. Thomas immediately asked about Askay's grandson, Akmal Joseph. Tom explained that he was planning to study water systems and well development in college so he could help impoverished peoples, especially those who lacked fresh water. His main focus would be the Native American situation on reservations.

"But I've heard of groups in Togo and Tanzania who needed that kind of expertise. There's a particular tribe of Bantus in Tanzania who are Catholics that I'm interested in," he said.

"You wouldn't be going to Africa to convert people, would you?" Hank asked.

"No, sir. I think the Church has already done a good job of that," he said.

"Because I kind of think of the term *Bantu Catholic* as an oxymoron," Hank persisted.

"Well, sir, that may be, but it was their choice. Anyway, I'm not the missionary type. I'll be lucky to learn enough Swahili or whatever language is needed for my work in Africa."

"Oh, I'd love to go!" Sunny broke in. "And I'm good at languages."

"You're hired, you Iroquois Catholic!" Thomas said.

"I guess my folks can't say no to that," Sunny added.

They ate spring lamb swimming in cilantro-mint sauce, baked root vegetables, and corn soufflé. Thomas had brought a chocolate cake that his mother had made.

"Have you chosen a college, Thomas?" Hank asked.

"Not yet, Mr. Rose. You know there are scholarships for Native Americans at almost all the state universities, but I want to be in a smaller environment with more emphasis on my unique field, perhaps more on geology and hydrology than football."

"Good thinking, son," Hank said. "I'd be glad to write you a letter of recommendation."

"I'd appreciate that, Mr. Rose."

After dinner, Thomas and Sunny played Scrabble, trying to create oxymorons with each other's words, not exactly following Scrabble rules. Then they went completely crazy using Spanish, and once in a while, Sunny would call to her father where he was reading the paper in the kitchen, something like, "What's that Swahili word for *rain* Askay taught you?"

"*Mvua*," he said.

"Oh, I knew I had those letters!" she cried.

Hank went into the living room. "You remembered that?" he said to his daughter who had pressed her four-year-old face to the window of her room in rainstorms, softly singing, "*Mvua! Mvua!*"

"I did," she answered.

It brought tears to Hank's eyes. She had never really known Askay, but she would always make Hank translate words she liked into Swahili. When guests left the ranch, and Hank said *good-bye* to them, Sunny would pat his arm and insist, "Askay word! Askay word!" She always seemed to understand how that African had helped raise her father.

"*Kwa heri*," Hank would answer.

"Oh, Daddy," Sunny was saying, "I hope someday I can remember everything from that time and nothing from the years in between then and now."

Hank noticed Thomas looking away, absently fingering his Scrabble squares.

"Hold on, you two! I have a surprise for you!" Hank said.

He went to his and Susan's bedroom where Susan was already turning down the covers and began going through a drawer in his night table where he kept personal mementos. There was that poem of his mom's. There, too, was Serena's white diamond and his grandmother's black diamond, the one she was given the day she and Grandpa Henry died in the plane crash. And there, what he was looking for, an old CD with a recording of the song "Almost Paradise."

He took it out to Sunny and Thomas and told them they could have a dance, that this was Julian and Serena's song they had danced to nearly every Saturday night their whole life together and maybe some times no one knew about.

"Oh, Daddy, you kept this?"

"I kept a lot of things. But I'm thinking I should share them, give them life again," he answered.

"Like you gave me life again," she said.

He nodded and slid the CD in the player. Then he returned to the bedroom and lifted Susan into his arms as the first lines flowed out with the rich melody into the room of their own dreams, their own secrets, their own heaven, which, for that moment, was all they needed.

The next day, Hank dug out the worn leather volume of Askay's memories from deep in a drawer where it had lain for a decade. What wisdom from the African might reside there? What point of view that could heal? And then Hank stopped suddenly before turning the first page and clutched the book against his heart. Hank was looking for answers in words he and Susan weren't sure were right for their daughter! Askay had been Catholic!

Hank slowly parted the pages somewhere in the middle and read—*the girl is beautiful, but Hank not know trouble where it be born, where it die. Hail Mary, full of grace* … He felt as if the Tanzanian was in the room speaking the words. Hank knew he would have to start at the beginning and read every line.

◄◄◄◆►►►

Summer again. Sunny turned thirteen. Hank believed things were better now. He and Susan would never know the child Sunny, but they could know the teenage Sunny and then the adult Sunny. They had time to give her whatever she wanted, whatever she missed in those years apart from them. He began to think that way about it. She had merely been *apart* from them, not *kidnapped*, not *molested*, for the love of God.

That summer was a time of peace. *Amani*, Hank thought as he watched their daughter doing ranch chores—taking care of her ten-year-old dog Paraíso and her grandmother's eighteen-year-old mare Paraíso, riding with friends, and doing her school projects. She stopped seeing Dr. Dan, promising her father that confession did more for her than *that shrink*.

Before school started the fall she would begin eighth grade, Sunny went to a week-long church retreat in the foothills of the Jarbidge Wilderness. Thomas was a youth leader, and several of her friends, even non-Catholics, attended for the camping experience. When she returned, she was distant and quiet. Hank thought she had a faraway look in her eyes as if the world in her vision was a different one from the one she stood in. It seemed as if their daughter had retreated to the shy, uncertain child that they found in Santa Barbara. Susan asked if something bad had happened on the trip.

"No," Sunny said. "It's all good. I saw Jesus in the woods."

"What did he say?" her mother asked.

"'Love thine enemy,'" Sunny answered.

"Oh, easy for *him* to say," Hank said.

"Not so easy, I think," Sunny said.

"Can you do it?" Hank went on.

"I don't think so," she replied, "but I'm going to try. My life, *this* life, depends on it."

And then Sunny was caught up in her second year of junior high. There were more homework assignments, more afterschool activities, and more friends to spend time with. Again she missed the fair, even though she had managed to learn a nice bridleless routine on Grey Girl with Dancing Horse's help. Susan and Hank didn't go either.

"I think I've had enough of that fair," Hank said as he and his wife sat on the porch swing where once Serena had told Liana she'd had enough of her, in so many words.

It was a late afternoon. The sky seemed to be darkening early, and the air was unseasonably cold. Hank pulled a faded red blanket over them, thinking of the irony of the color.

"I wonder where she is," Susan said. "Liana, I mean."

"I know who you meant," Hank said. "And, personally, I don't care. She can't harm our child again, or anyone else's, I assume."

"Henry, you have been a rock through all of this. I know you talk to Sunny about things I never could. I'm so grateful."

"Surprisingly, it's been easier than I thought it would be. I mostly listen. I don't judge … either of them, and that's hard. I don't know what *really* happened to her. I don't suppose we'll ever know. Father Azenwa probably does. Sometimes he looks at us with a very grave expression. I don't know what to make of it."

"Would he tell us if Sunny was in trouble?" Susan asked.

"I don't think so," Hank said. "We'll have to trust that she'd tell us."

"I wonder which is worse for us, having her missing or dead, or having her back with wounds that can't be healed," Susan said.

"Only you can answer that, my little Iroquois," Hank said.

He hugged her against him, and they watched, for perhaps the thousandth time, the last rays of the sun break through the stark fall clouds on the western horizon for a moment of brilliance in a gathering storm.

◀◀◆▶▶

Though in many ways a free spirit, open to new ideas and new friendships, Sunny dressed very conservatively and was seen bending over her rosary at a football game instead of dancing for the home team with the cheerleading squad she had worked so hard to join.

When Hank heard about that from the coach, he asked her later that night what was going on. "You know what, Dad? You can't believe how much energy it takes to find your place with the Holy Spirit. The cheerleading is really kind of silly in comparison." Her haunting, Iroquois face broke into an amazing smile. "And something else. Just listen. Carinne and Laurel and Randy all got confirmed this year at St. Mary's without me ever saying a word to them! Isn't that fantastic? The power of the Holy Spirit," she said.

Hank could see that she drew everyone into her sphere of confession and devotion. But he wondered if those classmates that followed her example could know what was churning in her heart, the small Flame that faced extinction in the breeze of memory.

One night, as her mother brushed Sunny's dark hair until it gleamed gold on black, she put her hand over Susan's hand that held the brush and whispered, "Mommy never did this … with the hairbrush." Hank stood in the doorway and heard what she said. Sunny gave him a look that asked, *Is this a piece of the puzzle you wanted?*

Hank said. "I'm so sorry, Sunny."

"Well, I guess this is one way of turning a bad moment into a bright moment," she said.

Because she had this way of transforming things, everyone wanted a piece of her—the track team (photos of her father crossing the finish line at some big event lined the trophy case at school); the drama club (she had a way of living every line that was given to her); the Native American dancers; and, of course, Father Azenwa. She was his shining example of Catholic virtue. She prayed and went to confession and to church two or three times a week. She sang in the choir and led the youth group Faith Council. The Roses asked each other if she would have been *this* Sunny if she had not been abducted.

◀◀◀◆▶▶▶

That winter semester, an older boy, a junior named Timothy Long, started walking her to class, carrying her books, and sitting next to her in church, but she insisted they were just friends. Another eleventh grader, Andrew Wescott, began hanging out with them, and sometimes the three of them would study at the ranch and then go for long hikes together. Susan heard them talking a lot about social issues, conflicts between science and religion, and their plans for the future. They never asked Sunny about her ordeal, and Susan supposed that was why her daughter was so comfortable with the boys. Andrew often got terrible headaches, and Sunny and Timothy would comfort him, putting cool cloths on his head or just holding his hands.

Susan thought it was so sweet, but she noticed things the three of them probably didn't. As beautiful as Sunny was, now taller than her classmates with a sinewy and haunting posture, Andrew only had eyes for Tim. When they came into the yard from a strenuous hike on Saturdays, Sunny would not be between them. Andrew would be next to Timothy, unfailingly. This did not bother Susan at all that the boy might be gay, but she dreaded the pain that could strike the three of them, the questions, the taunts, the sexual tension that might, to Sunny, feel threatening.

But she need not have been concerned. One afternoon, Sunny bounced in from a long weekend church youth-training session and announced, "I found out something fantastic! Andrew and Timothy don't have crushes on me! They like each other!"

Susan was so pleased that Sunny could just blurt this out, that she knew her mother well enough to trust she would have no problem with that fact, she said, "Why, darling, I wasn't worried in the least. I kind of knew that."

"You did?" Sunny said.

"I just hope you can all stay friends. I like both boys very much."

"No, no, you see, Momma, they can use me! They can pretend to be fighting over me. I can flirt with them. No one will have to know how they feel about each other!"

"But, Sunny, isn't the truth better in the long run?"

Her face froze. "I don't know," she said. "The truth can be a horrible thing. I think the secret will save them."

"You might be right, Sunny. What do I know? You kids do what you think is best, okay?"

"Thanks, Mom, really, thanks for understanding."

But Sunny told her mother one day, in an unusual burst of confiding in Susan, that Andrew's mother had said the oddest thing when the boy wanted to join St. Mary's.

"What? What did she say?" Susan asked.

"Mrs. Wescott said to Andrew, 'No son of mine is going to *that* church! That priest probably already has his eye on you!' Mom, what is she talking about? It makes no sense!"

"Oh, God, Sunny, this is a truth you don't want to hear," Susan pleaded.

"Yes … yes, I do! I *have* to know!"

"Sunny, first of all, I absolutely do not believe Father Azenwa would hurt Andrew. That was a crazy thing for her to say. But, honey, in the Catholic Church, there have been priests, very few, but still, some, who have molested young boys."

"Molested?"

"I'm sorry, Sunny, but it's true. If Andrew's mother finds out her son is gay and that he's going to church with Timothy, she'll blame the priest. We can't let that happen. Let's think what we can do."

"We have to tell Father A, he'll know," Sunny said hopefully.

"Don't you think Andrew and Tim should do that?"

"I guess so. But, Momma, what does *molest* mean in that context? I mean, really it seems bizarre."

Susan got up and went to the bookcase and came back with a dictionary. "I'm not trying to get out of telling you, my darling daughter. I just think it would be easier to read it than to hear it." And she put the book in Sunny's hands.

After a few minutes, Sunny closed the dictionary and made the sign of the cross. Her face was stone, but she said, "When boys have sex with boys, is that *molesting*?"

"No, Sunny. When two gay people have sex, or have those feelings, it's wanted by both, it's *normal* for gay boys or girls. But it's not normal for a priest, or any adult, to do sexual things to a young boy."

"Then it's not normal for a grown woman to do it to a little girl," Sunny said.

"That's the truest truth I know," Susan said.

"And you're right. I don't want to know," Sunny said. She ran into her room.

◀◀◆▶▶

Later that night, she told her father about Andrew and Timothy and what Andrew's mom had said.

"That foolish woman," Hank said, slamming his newspaper down on the coffee table.

"What can we do, Daddy?"

"We can stand up for those boys. They're two of the nicest boys I know," Hank replied.

"But, Daddy, do you think what they … want to do … is wrong?"

"I personally don't think so, but it's a controversial subject. Your own Church would call it a sin," he reminded her.

"A sin?" She seemed shocked. "No! It can't be a sin! They would be cut off from God!"

"Sunny, I don't think God cuts anybody off," Hank said but thought of Liana rotting in a cell someplace and hoped maybe the Catholic Church was right about this. But that would mean some sins were unredeemable, and he believed in redemption, if only for the unpredictable and often dangerous horses that entered the round pen and left new creatures. Suddenly, he didn't want to have this conversation with his daughter. What was done to her was not *sex* but violent abuse, but he didn't know how Sunny would reconcile it in her mind.

"Either he cuts people off or he doesn't. How is anyone supposed to know?" she asked with such determination. "You could do something … foolish, something you wish you could take back, and wham, God would be gone! I can't live like that!"

"Sunny, your grandmother Serena would say, 'God loves everyone … even Liana.' My mother gave to a woman, perhaps crazier than Liana, her dying wish."

"What was that?"

"To be buried here on the ranch. Her grave is out by Towering Peak. It's a long, long story and not like *your* story, but each person in that story found peace in the end. I believe Tim and Andrew will find that peace, and I believe you will too. That's the best I can say right now."

"Can you tell me about that other crazy woman?" Sunny asked.

"I can show you the words of a very wise man who lived through that time with Julian and Serena," Hank said. He left her for a moment and came back with Askay's thick journal. When he put it in her hands, he said, "This man was Catholic."

◀◀◀◆▶▶▶

After that day, as spring came again, Sunny spent almost equal time reading the Bible fanatically and the African's memoirs as if looking for all the answers to her endless questions. When Hank and Susan explained things in each one's point of view, she would say, "Those are your words, not God's."

She told her folks that she remained close to Timothy and Andrew. "We protect each other. Sex is not an issue. The boys hold my hand at school and then kiss each other in the barn after our homework is finished. It doesn't bother me. It has nothing to do with me," she assured them. But one Sunday, when the Roses went to St. Mary's for a friend's granddaughter's baptism, Father A changed things in a dramatic way.

"I have made a very difficult decision," the priest said to Hank and Susan privately. "I wanted you to know, so you could prepare Sunny."

The Roses waited for another blow to their tormented world.

"I have advised Timothy and Andrew to break off their relationship and that Andrew attend the Methodist church with his parents. Timothy can stay here in our congregation."

"And how does that help anyone but you?" Hank asked, feeling a bit defensive of the boys and mean. He knew it was beneath him and was immediately sorry.

Father Azenwa sighed and tried to answer. "My dear Hank and Susan, I'm doing it *for* the boys. When they are older, out of school, out of their parents' homes, they may find their attraction still valid and act on it. I will not love them any less. But even though I accept homosexuals, my Church does not, their behavior anyway. I took a vow to uphold the tenets of the Church. But if my parishioners or parents outside the Church thought I was promoting these boys' relationship—at what? Sixteen or seventeen?—I could lose my position here. The boys have agreed. They say you and Sunny are the only folks who know about them, and they care immensely for your family. They know something of what happened to Sunny and don't want her to be hurt by some kind of gossip, especially of a sexual nature."

"But she will be hurt by this," Susan said. "She will misunderstand an issue she's already having trouble with."

"Of course, I can't tell you what she says in confession, but I can assure you nothing of a sexual nature has come up," the priest said.

Hank thought even that might possibly have crossed the boundary of the confessional a bit.

"Father, thank you for this confidence. I believe the kids can handle it. Their friendship is very deep," Hank said, trying to soften his earlier demeanor.

"Well, I pray so. They are good for each other, I believe … and for the world."

12

◀◀◀◆▶▶▶

The purple crocus broke out of its white prison, and the sun blessed the dreary landscape with its warmth and hope. Andrew told Sunny he had decided to go to church with his folks and not spend so much time with Tim. She took it in stride until Timothy started talking about an older boy, a guy at college with a cool car, lots of money, and a dad who could take them anyplace in his airplane.

"What about Andrew?" Sunny asked.

"It wasn't working out. My boyfriend, Stuart, is Catholic, and his parents know he's gay. Much less hassle, girlfriend," Tim said. "And I love to fly."

"I thought you loved Andrew," she said.

"I do … I did … oh, Sunny, just leave things alone, okay?"

"Okay," she said.

She withdrew deeper into her dreams and memories. Andrew kept calling her, but she wouldn't come to the phone. She made Hank or Susan say she wasn't home or that she didn't feel well. She mostly rode alone and even ignored Dancing Horse's attempts to interest her in dressage or round-pen work with some horses from the Reservation that needed help. "I wouldn't be good for the horses right now," she told him.

Finally, one Saturday, the first warm day in the late spring, Andrew showed up at the ranch. Sunny was tacking up Grey Girl, and she went and caught Grey Boy, now nineteen but always up for a trail ride, and the two of them headed out for the Falls. It tumbled with snow runoff and the rain that had fallen higher up in the mountains. It was a hollowed space, discovered by Serena and Julian during their first few weeks together and reserved for family and special guests.

They sat on some mossy rocks and let their feet dangle into the expanding pool at the bottom of the draw. The water was cold. The hobbled horses wandered a bit, searching for new, green grass.

"Sunny, what happened? I thought we were friends," Andrew started in.

"We are ... but don't you miss Tim?"

"Yeah, I do, but when you're forced to make different choices, things change."

"Forced? You were forced?"

"I thought you knew. Father A said we were too young to be fooling around with forbidden things."

"Forbidden by whom?" she asked innocently.

"By the Church—Tim's Church—maybe mine too, and by God."

"God doesn't forbid love," she said.

"Sunny, God forbids the *sex*," Andrew said, trying to explain.

"That can't be!" she cried.

"But it says in the Bible, men shall not lie with men or women with women. God hates it. It's perverted."

"I never read that!"

"Well, it's true."

Sunny threw her arms around him and said, "Then let's love each other! Let's have sex. That will make everything right!"

He gently removed her arms but kept her hands in his. "It's not that simple, Sunny. Of course, I love you, but I don't want to have sex with you. I like boys. I like sex with boys."

"You like it?"

"It's the only thing I like. It's who I am, perverted or not."

"Even if God doesn't want you to like it?"

"God made me the way I am. If it's a sin, then too bad."

"Oh, Andrew, I could never be cut off from God!" Sunny exclaimed.

"If you ever had sex with a woman, you would be," he said.

Sunny jerked her hands from his and held them up as if fending off a blow. She choked helplessly as if those very words were strangling her.

"Oh my God, Sunny, I should never have said that. Oh, please forgive me," Andrew shouted after her.

But she was already unbuckling the hobbles from Grey Girl's front legs. She swung up on the mare and raced down the trail, blinded by tears and the darkest terror she had ever known.

◄◄◄◆►►►

That summer, when Sunny resigned from the Faith Council and didn't go to any of the camping retreats, Father Azenwa tried to talk to her. He drove out to the ranch to watch her ride, and then they sat on the observation deck watching Dancing Horse teach his daughter's black stallion the passáge.

"Such a magnificent creature, and that move, you can almost hear the music. What would it be?"

"Something from Respighi's *Ancient Airs and Dances*," she said without hesitation.

"All answers should come so easily," he said.

She didn't say anything.

"I don't see you with Thomas Heart-of-the-Hawk much anymore," he went on.

"He's off visiting colleges and dating a girl from the Reservation that I don't know. I do miss him," she said. "I haven't put up any posters lately. Even my folks don't understand how I feel."

"You are too young a girl to carry such a heavy load," the priest said.

"I want to see her," Sunny said.

"Who?"

"Liana," she said.

"Why?"

"I want to know if everything she did was just to hurt my father."

"What did she do?" he asked.

"I can't tell you here."

And so it was that a few weeks before she started the ninth grade, fourteen-year-old Marta Helen Serena Sun Rose stepped into the confessional at St. Mary's and opened the little window into the priest's ear. She had not spoken a word there for some weeks.

"Bless me, Father, for I have sinned," Sunny said clearly.

"And what sin is that, my child?" the priest asked.

"I had sex with a woman."

Father Azenwa crossed himself and faltered for words. He did not necessarily believe *being* homosexual was a sin, but what was done to Sunny surely was.

"Was it consensual?" the priest asked.

"I'm not sure what that means," Sunny answered.

"Did you both agree to … to touch each other?"

"No. I didn't want to do it, but I didn't stop her."

"Who, my child?"

"Mommy."

Dear God, he prayed silently. "Not your *real* mommy," he said.

"Not the mommy I live with now," she said through the curtain.

"What mommy?"

"The mommy I lived with for eight years."

"What did she do?"

"She put her hands … and *things* inside me."

"Did you enjoy it?" *What was he thinking! Of course she didn't enjoy it! God help me,* he said to himself.

"No," the girl said. "Sometimes it hurt, but sometimes, when she was gentle, I didn't mind. I let her. Is that being *consensual*?" Sunny asked.

"You must have been powerless to stop her," the priest said. "You would have stopped her, if you could, wouldn't you have?"

"I don't know," Sunny said in barely a whisper.

"What do you think God knows?" he asked.

"I think God knows my very soul, but he won't tell me."

Father Azenwa, almost for the first time in his priesthood, was at a loss for words. This child should be out riding in the sun, laughing with her many friends, singing in the choir, not sitting here in the confessional appalled that she might have *enjoyed* the touch of a woman, a woman who used her and hurt her, never *loved* her, as far as he knew.

"If you saw this … Liana, again, tell me what you would ask her?"

"If she ever loved me, if she thought anything she did to me was … normal or if it was just revenge."

"What you described to me was not normal," he said, wishing he could see the girl's face. "What if Liana thought something about it was?"

"Then I could hug people again and not be afraid of what I felt."

"Oh, Sunny, I think you need more than what I can give for this," the priest said.

"But I trust you," she said.

"I think you can trust *real* love to lead you where you're meant to be."

"And how will I ever know what's *real?*" she asked. "How does anyone know?"

"We can pray to know, child. That's all we can do. Shall we?"

And together they said *The Lord's Prayer,* slowly, as if each word were an answer.

"Your sins are forgiven," Father Azenwa said and opened the door.

She came out, but he saw that she wouldn't spare him. "Father … I want to go to the convent."

"Why, child?"

"Because I want to be the bride of Christ. He wouldn't hurt me. He would heal me."

"I believe that's true, my girl, but it is a big step."

"It's one that I have already made, in my heart. Will you take me to the convent?"

"Serena Sun Rose, I will not take you away from your parents again!" Father Azenwa said.

"I'll still see them, but I won't have to live in this world. I can't live in this world. I can't be touched. People are always wanting to hug me. I hate it."

"You mustn't have hate in your heart. How then can you love God?"

"I don't hate the people, just the touching."

"Not all touching is bad, Sunny," the priest said.

"But I don't know how to tell the difference. The Bible doesn't really explain it. One time ... I think I was nine, I'm not sure, Mommy—Liana—kind of danced with me ... in the shower. She had her hands, you know ... and after a while, it felt so good," she said.

"Sunny, sometimes your body betrays you," Father Azenwa said.

"What does that mean?" she asked.

"Sometimes your mind says *no,* but your body says *yes.* Sometimes you can change your mind, but you can't always stop what is happening to your body."

"But why did I stay so long? I could have run away!"

"Darling, where would you have gone? Someone meaner than Liana might have taken advantage of a lost little girl," he said.

"I just wanted to go to Nevada, and I didn't even know why. Now, I'm sure I want to go to the convent. God is leading me there, and *he* would never take advantage of me."

"Are you sure you aren't just looking for a place to hide from the world?" he asked.

"I've been hiding at the ranch all summer, and it hasn't done me any good," she answered.

"Sunny, go home and tell your mother and father everything you told me. Tell them your secrets. Your fears. Then we'll see," the priest said. He reached for her as he would any parishioner or friend, forgetting what she had just said about being touched, about everything, and she skittered away like a pebble on a steep slope.

◄◄◄◆►►►

Another year went by, and Sunny did not tell anyone her secrets. She rode her Arabian mare in the fair and won the English Pleasure and

Western Pleasure classes, something that had never been achieved by that breed in Nevada. She rode with such balance and light hands that her horse felt relaxed and comfortable. "If only life could be so easy," she said to her parents, handing them two big, silver trays and two long, blue ribbons. "I wish the lady with the horse on the beach could have seen me!"

She played Cordelia in the Honor Drama's production of King Lear to a standing ovation. The teacher told the Roses she could have a degree in the performing arts and do well in any acting endeavor. She was growing up way too fast for Hank and Susan. Thomas had come to that performance, and when he praised her, "You were amazing. You made Shakespeare accessible and wonderful!" she just shrugged her shoulders.

The only thing she really seemed to have her heart in was driving one of the trucks for the wranglers to roll out the winter grass hay for the cattle. One day, dragging in from hours of work in a raging blizzard, she said, "That was so good for me. I didn't think of Liana until just this minute!"

Hank admitted to her later that he still had dreams about *that woman.*

The next day, Sunny skied up to the old cabin in the canyon and laid one of her blue ribbons on her grandparents' grave. "Tell me about the locket," she said to her dad when she had stepped out of her bindings and climbed out of her down suit. She was barely in the front door.

"Not yet, Sunny … not yet," he said.

She helped plant the garden in the spring and in one corner of the half-acre ground uncovered an altar Askay had made where perhaps he had prayed, nursing the tender seedlings as they reached for the sun. *The African reached for the Son,* Sunny thought. Later, she pulled up weeds as if they were demons. Hank had to bring her in in near darkness.

"But I'm not finished yet," she protested. She raked feverishly at the curling stems and limp leaves. The dog Paraíso rooted in the dirt and carried old potatoes he found in his mouth over to Sunny and dropped them at her feet. She stopped and knelt down to ruffle the dog's coat and kiss his nose. "Let's go in, good boy," she said.

She let her parents see her cry one night when she couldn't work out an algebra problem. She called Thomas, even though she knew his girlfriend might answer. "Do you have time to help me with some algebra?" she asked him.

"I always have time for you," he said very softly. The girlfriend must have been in the room.

At the beginning of summer, Sunny packed for a weekend in the Jarbidge Wilderness. It was a Faith Council retreat, and even though she was no longer a member, she was invited because of her faith and her way of finding a scripture for every circumstance or spiritual need, except her own. She returned from that trip fairly calm. She moved with the grace of a dancer, a runner, a rider, doing chores or helping Luz with meals. She readily put her arm around her mother and the wranglers if she perceived it was a touch they needed. When Tyrone got burned with the branding iron, she quickly took him by the uninjured arm and called for Dancing Horse to come work his Indian magic.

She turned fifteen.

Her father told her that it had been a year of his mental crossing out of days from the time she was missing.

◀◀◀◆▶▶▶

Father Azenwa visited from time to time. It seemed to Susan that the priest always had a kind of questioning look on his face, but the subject of Sunny's missing years never came up. The Bible was never read aloud in Susan's presence, though she wouldn't have minded. *The Great Spirit belongs to all*, she thought. *His words must be in that Catholic Book too.* But no one ever asked her opinion.

She drove Sunny to school on the first day, as either she or Hank had always done, sometimes together, but that day he'd had to call the vet for a colicky horse. Her daughter said, "Bye, Mom," as she got out of the car and joined a few other tenth graders on their way into the main building. Sunny seemed subdued, anguished, as if that day was the end of something instead of the beginning. The tone in her voice had given her away.

Susan saw the poster as soon as she pulled back into the ranch yard. Hank was coming from the barn, so apparently he hadn't seen it yet, nailed to the front door and hand painted in huge letters.

I AM GOING TO THE CONVENT.

"Did you know about this, Henry?" Susan asked with tears beginning to form in her dark eyes.

"I had no idea," Hank told her. "Father A said something last year, but I didn't pay enough attention to it. Or I didn't want to hear it."

"What? What did he say?"

"Something like, 'I think we're losing her. This thing with the boys. It shook her. My hands are tied. The Church has positions on these matters.'"

"Henry, why didn't you tell me?"

"I talked to Sunny back then. She said she understood. She said there were all kinds of love in the world. She knew of three kinds herself and wouldn't judge any of them. I didn't think she was stressed enough to become a nun!"

"Okay, but she's been different this year, filling her life with friends and activities as if it were the last … oh my God, the last time she would be able to! Were we blind?" Susan became panicked.

"We just didn't want to see those subtle changes. We trusted she was getting better," Hank said.

"I don't think those changes were so subtle, Henry. I think we were asleep on our watch," Susan said.

"We had more guests last year. We bought more horses. We went back to *our* lives, the lives we had been leading while she was gone! What if she needed something different from us?"

"What if she needed us to be Catholic?" Susan asked, grasping at any ideas she could to explain this not-so-subtle poster.

"I don't think that's it, Susan," Hank said, staring at the poster that seemed to be shouting at them now.

"Should we try to keep her from going?"

"I think we have to respect this," Hank said.

"Respect all you want, Henry. I'm going to talk her out of it."

◀◀◀◆▶▶▶

Near the end of that day, Sunny got off the school bus and began the long walk down the driveway. Hank watched her come and said to Susan, "This feels like that time we talked about our missing child coming home and we wouldn't know who she was. Now it's happening."

"Don't try to stop me," she said when she reached them standing on the porch.

"Just sit down for a minute, darling," Susan said.

They all went into the kitchen and sat at the oak table where many grave decisions were made over the years.

Hank began, "Sunny, we've let you live to your heart's content, let you be Catholic, whatever you wanted—"

She cut her father off. "There's one thing you can't give me."

"What's that?" Hank asked, so mad at himself for letting her get that far down the Catholic road.

"Absolution," the girl said.

"There must be another way," Susan said.

"Not for me," she answered. "Anyway, it's a service community. I'll wear regular clothes, maybe just a head garment to signify my station. I'll have a new name, a Biblical name, but it won't be so different from the one you gave me. I'll be Sister Martha. I'll see you as often as I can, but I will be the bride of Christ. I will take a vow that can't be broken. I will erase the child that was taken from you by doing penance for her sins."

"Sunny! You have committed no sins!" Hank said, his anger rising at the Church that promoted this tenet, at least strongly enough to contort the thinking of this young, horribly abused girl.

"You don't know that," she said calmly. "Now please drive me to St. Mary's. Father A has promised to present me today."

"Can you do this? Are you old enough?" Hank wanted to know.

155

"Parental consent is best, but I can emancipate myself from you and go anyway."

"Sunny, do you love us?" Susan asked.

"Of course I do. But I don't love myself, and God doesn't love me."

"Who told you God doesn't love you?" Susan asked.

"God himself … in the Bible. I prefer not to quote chapter and verse."

"Did you ever talk to Dr. Dan about this?" Hank questioned her.

"I never mentioned it. He wasn't Catholic," she said, running the cross on the chain around her neck back and forth.

"So she wins again," Hank muttered.

"What did you say, Daddy?"

"Liana wins again."

"She's in prison for life. I hardly call that *winning*," Sunny said.

Hank just remembered his own mother had been emancipated from her parents, and had, quite literally, saved horses and humans on her chosen path, one she chose at age thirteen. How could he argue with this intelligent, faithful, generous daughter about *her* choices?

Sunny stood up. "Can I get my suitcase?"

Hank stood up and folded his arms over his stomach, grimacing a little.

"Daddy? Are you sick?"

"Yes. I'm sick over losing you again," he said.

"You're not losing me. You're letting me find myself. I … I can't stay in your world. It's too confusing. It's too painful. I wanted to go last year, but Father Azenwa said no. I'd have to be at least fifteen and give myself more time to pray and read about cloister life. The more I did that, the more I knew it was the right path for me. I'm really sorry. I understand that it's hard for you. But one thing, just think of this—I'll be safe."

She went to her room for the few things she had packed. On her way out, she handed her mother a card with the address of the convent neatly printed. She gave her father one of her own paintings—a young girl crouched in the center of a round pen. The hand that reached through the rails was the Virgin Mary's, and behind her was the shadowy figure of Jesus. Hank set it on the oak table and took her suitcase.

"I'll get the truck," he said.

"My Iroquois prayers are with you," Susan said.

"I'll take them, Momma. You know I will. God hears those prayers too," Sunny said. She looked back once and then went out to her father, who moved as slowly as he could down the drive and under the sign Rancho del Cielo Azul.

13

◀◀◀◆▶▶▶

S unny became Sister Martha. She wrote letters to her folks describing initiate life. "I follow the timetable to the letter—prayers, meals, classes, choir practice, confession, house duties, and service assignments. I go to shelters and Catholic youth camps. I say my rosary and light candles." But when Hank saw the scrawl *Sister Martha* at the end of each note, he couldn't believe it was his daughter. He still ached for the four-year-old he had held in his arms, teaching her the names of the horses, the parts of the saddles and bridles, the flowers of the desert, and Askay's roses in the garden.

Sunny finished high school in the convent and graduated in a class of one. Her parents were there and her old friend, Allen Bowen. He spoke to her softly after the brief event. "My little Rainbow, I would have taken you home with me if I had known what was happening to you."

"But then I wouldn't have needed God," she said simply.

She was in a full habit, and Hank could almost not bear it.

"How are my horses?" she asked.

"Rachel's on sabbatical from Harvard, and she's riding them and helping her dad out with his chores. He's almost sixty, you know," Hank answered.

"Is he still riding?" she asked.

"He looks the same as he did when he was fifteen," Hank told her. He pictured the handsome Indian on the bare back of a horse, in the arena or out in the desert, blending so with the horse that it took Hank's breath away. It's the way he pictured his daughter, wanted her to be riding as long as she could, not cooped up in a gray-walled convent, her seat bones on a hard wooden bench instead of the very much alive and supple spine of the horse. But these things he did not say.

"And my dog Paraíso?" she asked.

"He almost made it to fourteen," Hank told her. "He's buried with his family." He didn't add, *the ones Liana killed.*

"He was my best friend for most of my life," she said. "I guess I kind of let him down in the end. I couldn't even watch him die."

"You couldn't be everyplace, Sunny. Besides, we loved him enough for all of us," her father said. "Your mother did the smudging ceremony, but he watched for you near the end."

She crossed herself. "I guess I will make some mistakes, Daddy. I just hope the final thing I do will be right."

"The final thing?"

"With Liana."

"I hope to God you never see her again," Hank said, wiping his brow. Why couldn't she forget the damn woman?

"I guess God will decide that," she said. "Oh, what happened to Timothy and Andrew?"

"Tim's in California at UCLA. Andrew got a good job managing the feed store in town and joined St. Mary's," Hank told her.

"I hope he can be who he is in the Church he loves," she said.

Hank wondered if Andrew loved the Church as much as he loved the absent Timothy. Or if the Church would try to *pray away the gay* in him. But he also knew Father Azenwa was sympathetic to gays and hoped Andrew could keep his faith in spite of the emotional toll the rules of that Church could take. All of this brought up again his own mother's attraction to the woman Carla. He couldn't reconcile all the images yet—beauty, abuse, sin, desire, betrayal, rejection, love. His mother's love for the woman Carla seemed pure and sinless in the light of Liana's loathsome act. He would have to read that poem again. He couldn't believe the words could stand for so many things, but maybe that's what poetry was supposed to do, draw you into the world that was the most real for you, the most joyful, the most tragic.

Sunny said, "Dad, I've been painting. My style is so much like Great-Grandmother Helen's, and I only have that one watercolor you gave me when I went to the convent. I'll bring mine home the next time I come. I think I've improved since I did that one for you the night before I left."

The Roses had given their daughter the old, battered picture that had been on the wall of Miranda's prison cell and then in Liana's hands as she crept away from the ranch in the middle of the night after Hank broke up with her. Then it hung in the barn after his dad had recovered it at an auction years later. Each owner had seen herself in the frightened bronc and needed the outstretched hand with the gift of patience or understanding or love. Each owner had used the gift in a different way, and Hank knew the painting would go on speaking to people as long as it existed. Julian's mother would go on showing people a better way with her bold strokes and soft rendering of her own hand thrust through the rails of the round pen with the healing offering no one had thought to make.

◀◀◀◆▶▶▶

As the years went by, Susan longed for her child in a way she thought Hank could not feel because he had been allowed into Sunny's thoughts and emotions so much more than she had. Susan was still waiting for the little girl whose hand she had released on a bright fall day, whose little girl dreams she could never make come true. Having her safe in a convent could not fix the emptiness of those missing years when Susan should have been the one keeping her safe.

"Are you at peace there?" Susan asked the year Sunny turned twenty-one and took her final vows.

"As much as I would be anyplace, Momma. Sometimes when I'm singing or painting, I think I'm in a priceless universe. I feel joy. And then I remember."

"Remember what, my Serena Sun?"

"The price I paid."

"What will you do?" her mother went on.

"Serve God and pray for forgiveness."

"And what do you need to be forgiven for? What do you have to be ashamed of?" Susan asked, as she had many times before.

"That I will never tell," Sunny said.

It almost felt to Susan in those moments that her daughter had been abducted by the Catholic Church. But she knew that wasn't fair. Sunny was loved and honored and protected. She did good works. And Susan still believed her daughter did not cry.

◄◄◄◆►►►

Rancho del Cielo Azul stayed secure on its northeastern Nevada ground. People changed, and horses changed, but the sky still gave the Roses its lofty blue day after day, its incandescent sunsets and the beauty of silence in a troubled world.

One day, Tyrone, the old foreman, eighty-two now and officially retired, appeared at the ranch house door and asked if he could have Helen's sketch of Julian carrying the newborn calf out of the storm. "I'm just *borrowing* it," he said. He still rode some and always helped with roundups and guests at the tent-camp, playing his guitar and telling trail stories. But he never played "Almost Paradise" as he had for the young Serena Skye and Julian lost in the heady power of new love.

He smiled at Hank. "I remember that time Serena hung onto her new boss, your dad, all the way to the hospital after a rattler struck him and Julian gazing at Serena across the evening campfire or beckoning her to the dance. So many good things happened here, son, even to bad horses and bad people. We have to honor the good things."

"I know, Ty."

"I'm not so damn old that I can't remember the good times."

"We had a lot of good times, Tyrone. And we made it through the bad times. Don't you worry about us now," Hank said. He gave the old wrangler a couple of friendly slaps on the back and helped him off the front porch.

Then he saw Billy working in the round pen, handling the rope and the scared horse as Serena had taught him, speaking to the animal with the same reassuring voice and manner. He thought, *The good things live on*, and suddenly felt better about Sunny. His daughter was helping people in her own way, in a church or a homeless shelter or by a wilderness lake. She didn't have to be in a round pen to hold out her hand to the suffering or forgotten or abused humans in her charge. Sister Martha Helen Rose would find the path to reconcile the bad times with the infinite good that was in her heart.

He thought of Angie, who was in her seventies. She had moved to Carson City to be closer to a younger sister. Hank had given her his mom's twenty-six-year-old Akhal-Teke mare, Paraíso. She had been one of his folks' best wranglers and could give the horse the care she needed, taking the horse on short rides and offering more personal attention than Hank was able to do. It was a choice that came with great loss, and he had not been able to watch Angie load the mare in the trailer the day she left.

Hank told Susan all these new insights he'd had into the choices he had made and said perhaps they weren't as different as the ones their daughter had made, how he believed when Sunny discovered choices that led to her healing, they would all be healed.

"I can believe that," Susan said. "It's better she's alive and accepted by that Church than lost somewhere on the road with Liana or buried someplace we'd never see. I know I questioned this … this uncertainty and change that came over her in the last few years. But she has really grown up. She's alive and doing the will of God. If there is a God, he's ours as well as hers, and that has to mean something."

Hank hugged his Susan, his Iroquois talisman. His little, black rock talisman was now loose in his keepsake drawer—the stone with two *essences,* his mom had told him when he was a boy, an obsidian Apache tear found out of character on his Nevada desert far from its Arizona cliff home, just there at his seven-year-old feet, waiting for a Native American to tell him the story. Dancing Horse had said, "Those are the real tears shed by mothers and aunts and sisters of the Apache warriors who rode their horses off a cliff to avoid being captured by US soldiers." Hank had always dreamed of taking his daughter when she was about eight or so to that place in the Southwest and digging out some of those black tears.

Sunny had her gold cross; he had his black glass. Both called the pain of history to light. Susan hung onto the worn, stuffed Grey Boy, the talisman of her kidnapped child.

◄◄◄◆►►►

A few months later, after those inevitable changes at Ranch del Cielo Azul, the convent sisters were assigned a new program, visiting the women inmates of Nevada's State Prison. Sunny was gone from the area near her folks for days at a time. The nuns sat with each prisoner for thirty minutes, talking or praying or watching them pace the room, waiting to be released back to their cells. Some prisoners converted to Catholicism, but Father Azenwa said that that was not the purpose of their service.

"It is to teach you patience and humility. It is to teach you how to listen and give comfort where it is most difficult. It is to show you the poor and hungry of a different kind."

The nuns were paired with inmates by age, younger with younger, older with older, thinking conversations would start up more easily, needs might be met, but no names were exchanged. Each prisoner had a number and could tell the nuns as little or as much as they wanted about their incarceration. No one expected friendships, but no one knew Sister Martha Sun Rose. Friendship was the first thing on her mind. These women had committed crimes, sins, just like she had. She could learn from them how they lived with these deeds, how they talked to God, if they talked to God, and if they had found a way out of their emotional prisons. She had no idea what to expect, what to say to them.

The first woman she met was her exact age, twenty-two. "I left my child in a closed-up car," number 88 said right away. "It was 104 degrees, in Las Vegas. My baby girl died."

Sunny gripped the table between them, and speech unraveled in her throat.

The woman touched her shoulder. "Are you all right, Sister?"

Sister Martha mumbled, "I didn't die. I didn't die. I didn't die."

"Get her away from me!" the woman screamed. "Who the hell is she?"

The sister with the biggest heart and the biggest secret had to be taken away and counseled herself. Then Sister Martha curled up on her bed, feeling that hot car of so many years ago, feeling that thirst that had panicked her little girl's body, and praying for all she was worth that she could talk to these women.

In the motel that night, the mother superior came to Sunny's room.

"Why did you join the convent, Sister?" the nun who wore the look of many stories, many answers to this question, asked.

"To serve God."

"Not to forget what happened to you?"

"No … to be forgiven."

"Then you will have to put those things behind you. You will have to be strong."

But about some things, Sunny was not strong. Some stories might be too close to her own, and she wanted to flee from them, bury them. For penance, she fasted that night, and the next day she went back and asked to see the woman who had let her baby die in the hot car.

The minute the cell was opened, Sunny cried, "I beg your forgiveness, 88. I was left in a closed-up car when I was twelve during a heat wave. You took me back to that terrible day. I'm so sorry. I will pray for your child for the remainder of my days."

The woman said nothing but turned her head away. "Can I help you?" Sister Martha asked in a final attempt to make a difference in number 88's life.

The young woman slowly faced Sunny again. "Can you tell me what it was like, being in that car, in that heat? Did you cry? Did you suffer?"

And Sister Martha lied. "It was a long time ago, but I think I just got very sleepy. The warmth wasn't too bad. There was some shade on the seat from a big truck parked next to ours. I could breathe there."

"Yes! There was a horse trailer next to my car, and my … my Lisa was in the shaded part of the front seat!"

"God took care of her. You will be forgiven," Sister Martha said.

"Oh, thank you, Sister. I don't know if I believe all that, but it must have taken a great deal of courage for you to come back to see me. That has helped me more than any words." She wiped some tears from her cheeks. "Thank God someone found *you*, Sister."

After that incident, Sister Martha was allowed to go home for a few days. Her dear friend from high school, Thomas Heart-of-the Hawk, was leaving for Africa soon and wanted badly to see her. They had lost touch as the young Native American found his way in the world outside the reservation, going to university and studying the courses of his dreams—geology, hydrology, well construction, water purification and flow.

He came out to the ranch, and he and Sunny sat in the grandstand overlooking the round pen. Hank was helping a neighbor with a new horse. The gruella mare had been drugged when the man bought her and now stood stiff-legged and unyielding before the two cowboys.

"It seems so simple, doesn't it?" Sunny said.

"What's that?" Thomas asked.

"You put a little pressure on the horse or ask for something it doesn't know or want. When it gives just the tiniest bit, you release the pressure, praise the horse, or ask it to do something familiar so you can praise it again. See? Watch the horse change. I know it works with humans, but for some humans, the praise, the release, is not enough, and they slide back into … dangerous behavior. The horse rarely slides back if the handling is consistent. I don't know as much as my dad knows or his mother knew. I missed those years. But I can appreciate the idea. I've even used it a time or two to change someone's … direction," Sunny explained.

Below, Hank gave a hand signal, and the mare moved out to her left at a trot.

"But what's the final benefit of this?" Thomas wanted to know.

"The horse thinks what the human wants is the horse's idea."

"Oh wow" was all he could say.

A sudden breeze rattled a loose rail at the top of the arena. The horse swung her head around and looked at Sunny's father. *She looks to my father as I look to God*, Sunny thought, but she didn't tell Thomas that.

"Sunny? Or should I call you Sister Martha?"

"Whatever you're comfortable with."

"Come to Africa with me! I found the Bantu Catholics! You could serve them. The children need English teachers. The church needs a music director. What do you think?"

"I think I might go to Africa someday. But first I have to know why I was made to serve the whims of a woman named Liana. She has a hold over me still, because I can't put the things she did to me to rest. I can't hate it enough. I worry that I *liked* it. I don't remember liking it, but the woman had these … reactions. I need to know what it meant."

Her dad was riding the horse now with no rope or bridle on its pretty head.

"I've never told a soul this, Thomas, not even Father A."

"You know you can trust me, Sunny," he said.

"I do. And now you're going to Africa!"

"Can't you confess to Father A?"

"I've tried. Just before I say the words, he says, 'Do this, do that, your sins are forgiven,' and opens the door. It's like he doesn't *want* to know. He did hear me one time, but it made him very uncomfortable, and he said I needed more than he could give. He offered me prayer and sacraments."

"But that's his job," Thomas said.

"Maybe it shouldn't be. He's only human. I think I challenge his faith, because he can't find the *Catholic* reason to hear me out. Abuse is a sensitive subject, after all."

"Sunny, I'll hear you. I'm not afraid."

"Thomas, I don't think I can say the words."

"What about your mother superior or one of the sisters. You must have good friends there now."

"Yes, I've thought of that, but something is stopping me. I know I have to get over it, but it doesn't fit into a tidy, little box yet, you know, a container you can put on a shelf in your past and never look in again. Things are always spilling out where I can *see* them. And that shapes everything I do."

"Look at that!" Thomas cried.

The gruella mare was doing stock horse spins, one-two-three-four-five circles in each direction, still with no bridle. Hank could slow the circles down or speed them up at will. He switched his coiled rope to the outside hand each time to help the horse, but she had figured out what to do, and when the two of them came to a halt, the mare looked around at Sunny's dad as if to say, "Okay, what's next?"

Sister Martha and Thomas had dinner together, and then she walked him to his car. He put his arms around her, and she let him. "You know, I've loved you since the first day I came out to the ranch to tutor you, when you were barely twelve years old."

"I know," she said. "I had so much hope then. I wanted to be ... normal."

"What did you think was *normal?*" he asked.

"Letting my own mother hug me. Not having to check every single thing in my head with scripture. Not having nightmares that became *wet dreams,* for heaven's sake."

"Oh, Sunny, I wish you had told me," Thomas said.

"Well, I'm telling you now and sending you off to Africa!"

"And I'm sending you back to God," he said.

"It's where I belong, Thomas. He has something to show me, and it will be worth all the pain," she said.

He put his hand on her cheek and said, "Don't forget me."

◄◄◄◆►►►

It felt good to be back in her own bed. Sunny hugged Grey Boy and said her prayers. But she dreamed of the woman Liana hugging her, not always meanly, sometimes as though Baby were a great treasure to be cherished and saved.

Before she left, Hank told her he and Susan had started going to St. Mary's. "It's mostly so we can hear news of you," her father admitted.

"That's as good a reason as any," Sunny said.

She felt more confident going back to the prison. She would not let the inmates' stories destroy her hard-won stability. She took her place at the meeting enclosure. There were no windows. Everything was gray, like storm clouds. Some of the furniture was bolted to the floor. Sister Martha wondered if God could even be in the room.

Number 49 was brought in. She was older than Sunny, about thirty, a black woman with horrible scars down part of her face and left arm, three fingers missing from that hand.

"Meth lab blew up," she said without any introduction.

"Oh, was anyone hurt?" Sister Martha asked.

"Besides me, ya mean? My boyfriend was hurt real bad. He dead."

"I'm sorry."

"What you sorry for? Ain't none of your business," number 49 said matter-of-factly.

"How long will you be here?"

"Dunno. Long as they need me to clean toilets, I guess. It hard sometime, with my arm 'n' all."

Sunny was taking notes.

"What'cha doin'?" the woman asked, leaning over toward the nun. The guard pulled her back roughly.

"That's not necessary," Sunny said to the bulky, uniformed woman.

"Sorry, Sister, them's the rules," the guard said.

Sunny told the burned woman she was writing the prisoner's number and ways to help her.

"I don' need no help from you."

"Would you like a different job?"

"Yeah."

"Well then. What do you like to do?"

"I like to cook."

At once, they both broke into helpless laughter.

"You all right, Sister," number 49 said when she could speak again.

Sister Martha got her a job in the kitchen.

◄◄◄◆►►►

Number 102 came in in a huff. "I shouldn't be here!" she said breathlessly. "Can you get me out?" Another black woman with big, frantic eyes. She slammed her hands on the table as she sat down.

"Why are you here?" Sunny asked.

"They said I robbed a liquor store! I saw this lady runnin' out. She banged into me, and I saw her clear as day. She kinda look like me, slender an' all, but anyway, I went on in an' pick up some six-packs. Suddenly the po-lice were there grabbing *me*. I had just cashed my man's paycheck, so I had a couple a hundred bucks in my purse. They say, 'Where you get all that money if you din't rob this store?' I say, 'I got mine legit. Why aren't you chasin' that other gal?' They make me sign somethin' sayin' I was a witness, come down to the station, but it turns out I signed a *confession!*"

"Didn't you read what you signed?"

"Well, I jus' believe them. I *was* a witness. I'll never forget that face. Please help me, Sister. I got two kids at home. Husban' split after I was jailed. Can't afford no babysitter. They mostly alone."

"How old are they?" Sunny asked.

"Four an' six. The girl should be in school. She smart. Jus' turned six though. Have to look after her little brother."

"I'm going to get some childcare for you and see about your release," Sunny promised her.

"Oh, thank you, Sister. God bless you."

It meant so much to Sunny, that blessing, because it came from the heart, not the usual *expected* blessings of priests and bishops.

At three o'clock that day, Sunny called her father. "Dad, you have friends in Winnemucca, right?"

"Yes, honey, what's wrong?"

"Oh, nothing with me. I've got a prisoner whose children have no one in the home taking care of them. They're four and six. I think I can get the woman out of lockup, but it might be a week or so. Can you find someone to help? Here's the address."

"I'll try, Sunny," he said.

By four o'clock, Hank called his daughter. "Okay, I hired a rancher's wife who I'll pay for twelve hours a day. She has a friend that's volunteered to care for the children for six hours, and the prisoner's mother agreed to stay for the remaining six hours. I can't do this a hundred different times, Sunny, but I couldn't leave those kids alone. I just couldn't."

A sketch artist came to the prison, and number 102 provided enough details to reveal the face of the robber, and it was circulated throughout Nevada. Sister Martha didn't have much hope for *posters*, but in less than a week, the woman was caught shoplifting in Safeway, and number 102 was set free.

Sunny called her dad back and almost cried when she heard his voice. "If I were a believer," he said, "I might see *someone's* hand in this, but I mostly see your hand."

"I know, Dad. I was just desperate to do some good here, and I believed she was innocent."

"Don't they all say that?" Hank asked.

"That was the first one, and she *was* innocent," Sunny reminded him.

The sound of her father's voice so gentle, so *normal*. Her life had never been normal, like these women, most of them, trapped in some kind of emotional whirlwind, abused and neglected. Many were there because poverty drove them to pursue illegal methods to survive; many lacked the education to fit into the job market; many were addicts hanging onto the only thing that got them out of bed in the morning—their next fix. Sunny became counselor and priest and friend.

One woman had threatened her husband with *his* gun. No signs of domestic abuse. *Right*. Another had stolen baby formula from a drugstore. Another had slashed the tires on the car of a social worker who had come to take away her children. There were bizarre cases as well. Someone had killed two hunters standing over the carcass of a young wolf, five puppies hiding and mewling in the undergrowth. The babies were gone by the time the authorities arrived. One inmate dumped the body of her stepfather in a well after feeding him rat poison in his favorite goulash. He had been raping her her whole life. She was nineteen. The man died *in* the well, shouting feebly for help while the girl sauntered off to freshman English at the local college. One had kidnapped a two-year-old boy after losing her child to meningitis. The boy was the same age and had the same blond curls.

But Sister Martha soldiered on. She arranged for good lawyers, wrote to family members encouraging them to visit the inmates, and even made up anonymous care packages to give the women from time to time. She was discouraged from doing this by her superiors, but it didn't stop her. Sunny felt as if she were scrambling down a path to her own redemption. She didn't believe she was saved just because the Church said so, just because a priest heard her confession every week and she consumed the essence of the risen Christ in every communion. She began to have a following. The prisoners requested her, would wait in a long line just for a few minutes with her. Then as they told their stories, Sunny would have to hold up her hand to the guard; they needed more time.

Sometimes the inmates' stories, if they were explicit enough, made Sunny think about sex. She couldn't imagine ever wanting or doing such things. The thought of people's hands and body parts here and there was so distasteful to her that she prayed with a vengeance to have those images swept from her mind. And yet, *and yet*, she remembered that very, very, very few times she had felt something like pleasure roll through her maturing body in the later years of her captivity. She hated it, but it was true. The exact thing that had aroused her she couldn't name. It was secretive and damning and magnetic at the same time. Her dreams were plagued with collages of long roads, deserts and forests, and miles of ocean breakers with her wrist bound to some part of the car, eroding the joy of learning new words and places, leading her ultimately to steamy rooms where she writhed in agony under the smothering red snow of Liana's hair.

At the bare table one morning, number 56 sat down, and Sister Martha listened to her damaging tale. The young woman was twenty and had killed her father. When the man was drunk, he beat her mother, who was unable to stand up for herself, severely compromised by MS. The daughter had called 911 several times, but her mother wouldn't press charges, saying it was her fault, that she had been too tired to fix dinner or iron his shirts. The girl's father had a permit for a handgun, and when she was nineteen, number 56 went to a shooting range and learned how to use it, placing it carefully back where she found it. A few months later, her father's rage turned to her. She wouldn't tell Sister Martha what he said or did, but the girl went to the desk drawer where he kept the gun and came back and shot him, one bullet straight to the heart. Her mother was languishing in a nursing home, and number 56 had only served a few months of a fifteen-year sentence. The judge said because she took shooting lessons, the crime verged on premeditation.

She was a pretty girl, with soft, brown eyes the same golden brown of her hair and a slight but curvy frame. She said the bigger inmates mostly pushed her around. She was scared to be alone with any of them. She'd heard that there was an older woman who said when number 56 walked by in the yard, "Hands off. She's mine. That's my baby."

Sunny grabbed number 56's hands—against protocol—and said, "Tell me her name."

"I can't, Sister. I'll really be in trouble."

"I'll see what I can do," Sunny promised.

That night, Sunny called her father. He answered on the first ring, "Hank Rose."

"Daddy?"

"Everything okay?"

"I'm not sure. Where's Liana?"

"I think she's in California. The extradition was taking some time."

"Can you find out?"

"Why? Sunny, what's going on?"

"I think she's here."

"Oh God. Sunny, you have to tell someone."

"It's just a feeling. I could be wrong."

"God, I hope so," Hank said. "I'll get back to you."

◀◀◀◆▶▶▶

At Rancho del Cielo Azul, a scrambling noise brought Hank outside soon after the call from Sunny. He didn't see anything at first but then noticed some movement. In the yard light, he saw a bright red desert fox disappear around the corner of the barn with a cottontail in his mouth. He went back in the house, chilled.

It was too late to call any officials on Liana's case. Hank paced the room for a few minutes and then sank wearily into Julian's easy chair. He picked up Askay's diary from the coffee table and turned to the part he'd been reading—*Akmal Joseph come. I feel Tanzania in his arms, see Tanzania in his eyes. He never love Roses as I. Too much Africa in heart. Very much serve them, not able love them. My great sorrow. Boy not Catholic. Not knowing of Holy Spirit, of grace. But good boy. Grace be learn from Serena though she not Catholic. God understand this. I not. Just watch her. Watch spirit in round pen fill hearts—horses, husband, mad woman, cowboys. Her own son not see. Son will suffer.*

Hank couldn't read any more right then. *Son will suffer.* He remembered riding in the round pen as a child but not believing in the ultimate power of the lessons there. He got attention from his mother. He learned skills. He was happy. But he had missed the magic, the grace, and Askay had known this.

Susan stood in the dimly-lighted doorway of their bedroom. "Can't you come to bed now?" she asked. "What is that you're so deep into reading?"

"A journal Askay left me. It's kind of like the Bible. I don't mean as profound or holy, of course. I mean you can open it to any page, and there's wisdom or the answer to a question or something that touches your heart."

"Show me," she said.

So Hank put his hands randomly in the thick volume and opened it again. He read the first words he saw—*Native Americans in Hank's life save him. He must follow.*

"Oh wow," Susan said. "How far back does this writing go?"

"Back to his life with Henry and Helen Rose before my father was born."

"May I read it?"

"Of course, my little Native American!" Hank answered. "But right now I'm going to let you save me from a certain longing."

"I can do that, my husband," she replied. She took his hand, and they walked slowly through the darkened house to their place of love and grace.

14

◄◄◄◆►►►

S ister Martha started having trouble eating and sleeping, so she wasn't sent to the prison with the other nuns for several days. She read her Bible. She turned often to Romans 5 and ran her fingers over the comforting words—*We rejoice in our sufferings ...*

She had begun to think of Liana as almost a fiction in her life. Sunny's reality was her service to the women of the prison, figuring out what they needed, praying for them, and listening to the suffering that poured out. She had not quoted that verse to any of them. It seemed to have been written for her eyes alone. Now she was called to prevent Liana, or someone like her, from molesting another *baby*.

The twenty-year-old was as vulnerable as the four-year-old in this setting. What could Sister Martha do? Then she had a disturbing thought. *Sunny would do an entirely different thing than the Sister Martha I am now. Who am I?* She had asked that question many times over the years. An abuse victim? A nun? A daughter? A horsewoman? A healer? A protector of number 56?

She grew thin. She spoke to no one. Father Azenwa asked for her confession, but she had none to give. She slept little. She plotted her retaliation. *She cried.* Sister Martha cried. Sunny remained stoic behind the curtain of the missing years. The mother superior told her she would give her a few more days and then would send her back to the convent for further prayer and reflection.

"No!" Sister Martha cried. "I must go back to the prison. There's someone I have to save!"

"Sister, you must leave the saving of the other to God and save yourself."

"You don't understand. God has nothing to do with this," Sunny said.

"Perhaps you were not ready for this vocation, Sister."

"There have been many things in my life I was not ready for. But here I am, and I'm going to stay until I know what I have to do, no matter what God wants." She whispered these last words.

After several days became two weeks, Sister Martha opened the door of her motel room to the face of Hank Rose. "Sunny, please don't let this assignment destroy you," he said.

"But, Daddy, I love the work! I'm a talisman for these inmates. I'm a safe place for their stories, their fears. I'm the only one who gives them hope. I haven't even told them that line from the Bible, that *hope does not disappoint us.* We're not supposed to evangelize here. But they accept something about hope from me! I'm trying to get stronger so I can get someone to safety."

"But, Sunny, where is your safe place? Where is your hope?" her father asked.

"For Sister Martha, in the Catholic Church. I have no doubts there."

"For Sunny Rose?" Hank asked.

"Far away from here. In another time," she said.

"Speaking of another time, I brought something for you, something from a long time ago. It touches what happened to me ... and maybe to you. It touches what happened to your grandmother Serena. I've read these words a hundred times. I love them, but there are questions with no answers, and there are answers to unimaginable questions. Just remember this—Serena knew how to find the *center,* with horses, with humans, with her own heart. This might help you."

And he handed her the scrap of paper with the entire poem scribbled out.

I have danced in the red snow, she read silently.

"Oh, Daddy, did Serena really write that?"

"I swear, honey."

"Do you understand it?"

"I'm trying to."

"But *I* said that … about Liana. How many meanings can one line have?"

"Hmm. Read the rest."

Her eyes skimmed the faint writing, line by line. Her hand flew to her mouth a couple of times. The beautiful and frightening words soared and then fell into her heart. She imagined her grandmother Serena writing the lines, going back and refining them, pulling out their power, struggling with their myriad meanings, as she must have done in the round pen going back time and time again to the mind of the horse and helping it find the answers it needed.

I have danced in the red snow
where the spring has frozen
where she finds me open
I do not flee
with my fresh wounds.

I feel her hunger
chance that dangerous ground
put my paws in her traps—
those lonely promises
that glint in her eye
at how I languish.

I am the bait
that melts the ice
in her hunter's sights,
But her arrows fey—
come sigh kiss cry.

And I go down to that little death
falling
falling
no dance left
her fingers locked on my spine
her strong jaw
gnawing on bone.

Those traces of crimson
floating the white tide?
It's only my heart
unconsumed.

When she finished, she looked at her father. "Has Mom read this?"

"No. I don't think my mother wanted anyone to read it except the person it refers to. I felt guilty the first time I read it years ago."

"Who is this about? Should I know?"

"It's about a woman named Carla."

"Oh God, the locket! I saw it out on the gravestone. It's the two of them!" Sunny said. She crossed herself and wilted into the nearest chair. And then she whispered, "It's really beautiful. It's beautiful and terrible and oh so true. *It's only my heart / unconsumed.* She wanted it. She wanted that woman. My grandmother, after whom I was named, loved a *woman.*"

"But she chose my father. She chose Julian, and everyone felt blessed when they saw them together."

"I didn't have a choice, Daddy, and I was not blessed. However, that may still come," she said.

"I know, sweetheart. But you have a choice now. Come away before Liana finds you again."

Sunny glanced down at the poem. "*I do not flee with my fresh wounds,*" she quoted. Then she began laying out her habit, smoothing the black cloth of her head garment, gathering her Bible and her notes she had made about the prisoners.

"Where are you going?" Hank asked. His eyes widened in alarm.

"Back to the prison, to … *chance that dangerous ground,* with the faith of the grandmother I never knew."

◀◀◆▶▶

Sister Martha entered the prison that afternoon and asked to see number 56. The nun waited in the gray room for the young inmate, hoping the pretty twenty-year-old was still all right. And then there she was, rushing into the room. Relief was written on number 56's face. She reached her hands out and then jerked them back quickly, as if remembering the rule not to touch the nuns.

"Sister! We all missed you! Number 14 finished that book you gave her. She wants to talk to you about it. And number 3 found out you can sing. She thought maybe you'd help us start a choir!"

"Yes … I could do that. But how are you, 56? Anyone bothering you?"

"Oh, no. I hear things, but no one's tried anything. I've learned how to avoid the bad gals."

"You'd tell me if someone … hurt you," Sister Martha said.

"Yeah. Hey, could you get me a book? We don't have a very good library here."

"What do you like?"

"I like animal stories but not those real sad ones."

"I'll bring you *Winter Dance* by Gary Paulson. It's about a reporter who decides to run a team of dogs in the Iditarod. You'll laugh and cry, but it's a wonderful read."

"Thanks, Sister. And will you pray for me?"

"Certainly."

"You know, there's a lady here they call the *baby-snatcher.* I don't know her number, but she scares me."

Sister Martha swallowed hard and grasped with one hand the steel leg of the table that was bolted to the floor. She said, as calmly as she could, "I'll take care of it."

That was enough for Sunny. Even if it wasn't Liana, it was someone just as brutal. She felt her heart quiet at the prospect of putting an end to everyone's pain. But a few more inmates crowded the doorway when they learned of Sister Martha's return, and she felt called to hear more of their stories.

Number 32 hadn't heard from her twin brother for weeks. He had a drug problem, and the woman was afraid he had *gone back to his old ways* without her around to keep him straight.

"I was trying to get a refund from the dealer. We could use the money. I had the pills in my purse. But the guy was an undercover cop, and he didn't believe me," number 32 explained.

"Do you remember his name?" Sister asked.

"I think it was Holloway, but that might not be his real name, you know."

"I'll talk to him," Sister promised.

Number 9 stormed in. "Sister, I told 'em I could not eat meat! All's that's left on the plate without the meat is some french fries and maybe a scoop of Jell-O. I'm starving!"

Sunny called down to the cafeteria. "This is Sister Martha with the Prison Outreach. Could you offer more vegetarian dishes to the inmates?"

"You're kidding," a harsh voice said.

"I don't kid," Sister replied.

"Well, it might cost more," the cook said.

"I'll pay for one of my women to have more vegetables and salad," Sister Martha told him.

"You'll pay for one of these *criminals?*"

"*Whatever you did for one of the least of these ... you did for me,*" she quoted from Matthew 25:40.

"Are you preachin' at me, Sister? That's against the rules."

"I'm not known for following the rules, sir," she said. "Just repeating the Lord's words."

"Well, my uncle has a stand at the farmer's market. I could pick up some things. Uh ... no charge, Sister."

Sister Martha made the sign of the cross and said, "May God bless you."

◄◄◄◆►►►

Sunny had forgotten how exhausting all this problem-solving was. Just because she decided to do something for an inmate didn't mean it happened overnight. There was paperwork for the prison administrators, the social workers, and even for her own order. But it felt good, like a penance that clears your soul.

She contacted Detective Holloway later that week. She discovered he was Catholic, so she appealed to his vows of not bearing false witness. She assured him the woman he had captured undercover had shown no signs of withdrawal from drugs and had competently read a page of music for choir auditions, no addict's brain there.

Her brother hadn't contacted her for a suspiciously long time, and perhaps the officer had incarcerated the wrong twin. He listened politely.

"I might be able to do a little more investigating on the matter," he said.

"Thank you, Mr. Holloway, and God's blessings on you," Sister said.

Several days and nights passed. Sunny was able to sleep again. She dreamed of the horse on the beach, the exquisite and powerful motion of his four legs finding their balance in the turbulent surf. She gathered the strength of the horse for what she must do next and woke up smiling. Her Iroquois mother would be pleased at Sunny's choice of the horse for a spirit guide, even if it was only a dream.

Number 11 asked to meet Sister Martha the first day the woman was imprisoned. The overweight Latina hardly gave Sister Martha time to greet her. "I don't want to talk about myself. I got to tell you about something I saw this morning right after pat-down. You got to do something, Sister!"

"What? What did you see?" the nun asked.

"I saw a skinny broad with her hands on a young gal's breasts, pushing her up against the wall in the rec room. That ain't right," number 11 said. "If I tell the guards, I'll just be the new rat in the building. You got to do it!"

"I'm aware of the situation, 11," Sister said. "But is there anything I can do for you?"

"Nah. I'll be okay. I can throw my weight around a little bit. I did some shoplifting, but I ain't bad. I was jus' worried about that gal. She looked so scared."

"Thank you, 11. You did the right thing telling me," Sister Martha said. But she hadn't really figured out what to do. Just a confrontation may not be enough. And if it was Liana, did she want her to know she was there?

Then the sisters had a day off. The prison was in lock-down to do a search for drugs and other contraband. Sunny and Justine, an older nun that Sunny had come to know fairly well, went to a rose garden in a nearby park and walked slowly among the magnificent blooms, marveling at the variety and beauty of the colors and shapes. They sat on an antique, wooden bench and had a small lunch. Suddenly, Justine pointed to a patch of roses they had not noticed before.

"Look, Sister, there, in the center, is the color of one of my inmate's long hair! She has a little gray, but you can tell it was that bright color once."

Sunny stared deep into the showy bushes. Sister Justine was pointing at a flaming red, a color Sunny hated, that rapacious red bursting from the *rose* of her own name. She tried to control herself. *It couldn't be this easy,* she thought.

"Sister, what's her number?"

"I think she's number 4," Justine answered.

Sunny sat very still for a moment. Her heart was in her throat. "When do you see her, Sister?" she was finally able to ask.

"Let me think. I believe Thursday."

It was Monday. Sunny trusted Justine but didn't want to alarm her. She put the question to her as casually as she could. "Sister, could I trade with you on Thursday?"

"That's an unusual request, Sister. I'm not sure Mother will allow that."

"We can wear our habits that day. No one will suspect anything. Some of the inmates say they like us in our Catholic clothes."

"Yes, I've heard that," Justine said hesitating. "May I ask why you're interested in number 4?"

Sunny said simply, "I think I know her." This was pretty safe, because Justine didn't know everything that had happened to Sunny. But it was frightening too, because what would she say to the woman who had haunted her for many years beyond those eight of her damaged childhood? She closed her lunchbox and moved her hands along her rosary, sometimes the only thing she wanted to touch. Then she stopped with a shudder. At that moment, she was not Sister Martha. She was Marta Serena Sun Rose going out of the fairgrounds to see a puppy, holding a stranger's hand.

The week dragged. Sunny picked at her food and did not open her Bible. She read Serena's poem over and over. Every line had endless meanings, but one seemed to foreshadow the coming scene—*I am the bait that melts the ice in her hunter's heart.*

She called her father. Hank answered. "Daddy, will you still love me if I do something foolish?"

"You know I will. Is it dangerous?"

"Only for my soul," she answered.

"You found her?"

"I'm not sure. Maybe. I feel so *apart* from everyone—the sisters, my priest, you, God."

"Sunny, did you know you were born three weeks after my parents died?"

"No."

"You were a part of *my* life when my life was most ravaged. You brought my father's brother back to me. You brought my joy back. You saved your mother after she was told she couldn't have children. No one knows that. I'm telling you so you will know some things from which you will never be cut off."

"Liana cut me off for eight years!"

"She never cut you off from our love."

"Okay, Daddy. I have to go now. Don't worry about me. You … helped me, really," Sunny said softly and turned off the phone.

When Thursday came around, Sunny's habit hung loosely on her already thin frame. Sisters Martha and Justine arrived at the prison, looking the same in black cloth and head pieces that shadowed their faces. Neither hair color nor eye color could be seen in the dim prison light. Justine turned toward Sunny's room, and Sunny toward Justine's. No one noticed.

Sunny sat in the steel chair waiting for number 4. She could not think of a single Bible verse. She was thrown back to the first day she clearly remembered eighteen years ago, the day she dialed the zero on the telephone and told the woman she thought she was with the wrong mommy. She felt again the terror of being alone in that cold, dirty trailer, waiting for the wrong mommy to return, wondering what terrible things she would think of to do to her. And then, a line did come into her head, but she flung it away. *Sorry, God,* she said silently. *Today, the vengeance is mine.* She felt for a moment like that little girl handcuffed to the back of a smelly van, anticipating a slap or later a caress that confused her still. She almost hoped it was anyone but Liana. To *dance in that red snow again* would be to have her heart consumed.

She heard the woman outside. "I don't feel like no religion today."

The guard opened the door. An aging, red-haired figure, as tall as Sunny remembered, stood in the doorway. "This isn't Justine," she said, sounding peeved.

"We don't care who it is. Just give her five minutes," the guard demanded.

The woman slid into a chair opposite Sunny and drummed her fingers on the table between them. "Well, let's get this over with," the inmate said.

And Sunny looked up into the eyes of her abductor. "Hello, Mommy," she said.

Liana's eyes narrowed, and a spark of alarm came into them. Then she stood and flung her chair back, one that had not, unfortunately, been bolted down. "You!"

The guard pushed number 4 down, and Sister Martha crossed herself.

"I'm not talkin' to you!" Liana said.

"You don't have to talk, just listen. You know that pretty young gal who killed her father in self-defense? If you lay a finger on her, I'll make your life miserable. Besides, isn't she a little *old* for you?"

"I don't know what you're talkin' about!"

"I thought you liked them to be *babies* and vulnerable," Sunny said.

"Why, Sister, that doesn't sound like a bride of Christ," Liana said, recovering her usual bravado.

"Right now, I don't feel like one. Right now I feel like Serena Sun Rose, kidnapped child of Hank and Susan Rose."

"A nun! For God's sake, Baby, get over it," Liana spit out.

"Get over God? Or get over you?"

"Both, if you want my opinion."

"Your opinion means nothing to me, but you'd better hear what I'm saying. I can make things so much worse for you."

"How?"

"I never told anyone what you did to me."

"It wasn't about you. I was trying to hurt your father!"

"But you *did* hurt me," Sunny said as coldly as she could. "What do you think all these inmates who like me now would do to you if they found out some of the things you did to me?"

"Why, Sister, don't you believe in forgiveness?"

"God may forgive you, but I'm not there yet."

"Oh, c'mon, Baby, you enjoyed it, just a little, didn't you? Those baths? You would be such a clean Baby," Liana hissed, rubbing her hand on the table in a suggestive way.

"Then why do I still feel so dirty, Liana?" Sunny used her real name purposely.

"You can't say my name! It's against the rules!"

"Since when do rules mean anything to you?" Sunny asked.

"Since your father kicked me out of his life! We had *rules*. We made promises!"

"You killed his dogs," Sunny said, her anger rising again.

"Yeah, and I saved one for him. He has Paraíso's grandson now. That's a good dog!"

"It's a good *dead* dog. But at least he was loved."

Neither one spoke for a moment. Their time was almost up. But the conversation was not over.

"So do you go to confession and everything, Baby?"

"I'm a Catholic. You figure it out," Sunny answered.

"Boy, I'd like to be a fly on that wall," she said.

"It wouldn't be anything you don't already know," Sunny said.

"I can't figure why you became a nun. Are you sleeping with one of these sisters?"

"Liana … go to hell," Sister Martha said.

The mommy of old grabbed her, still so strong, and seethed, "Not without you, lil' Baby! Not without you!"

The guard rushed the inmate out and left Sister Martha staring at the bruise on her arm, aware now of the cold steel beneath her, the hot blood in her cheeks, the overwhelming guilt that she could not do what God wanted. She could not love her enemy.

◄◄◄◆►►►

Later, the mother superior admonished her. "What were you thinking, Sister Martha?"

"I had to look her in the eyes to see if I still hated her," Sunny said.

"And what did you find?"

"I hated that she could still be doing the awful things she did to me. One of my inmates, number 56, has been threatened by Liana—sorry, number 4. I was just doing my job, Mother."

"I think it's God's job to protect his children."

"Then I guess he wasn't on the job when that woman took me! When that woman *molested* me!" Sunny said the word she had never been able to say.

"I grieve for your pain, truly, Sister Martha, and I had no idea … that woman molested you? I had only been told you had been kidnapped and then reunited with your family many years ago. I can see you are still greatly troubled and angry about this," her superior said, "but you must leave the judgment to God. Now, go to your rosary. You must not leave this enmity in your heart. Do penance for your unfortunate words to the prisoner. There you may find peace," she said and made the sign of the cross over Serena Sun Rose.

But Sunny could not pray. She thought she would feel more bitterness after facing Liana, but she felt nothing, and that was the worst feeling of all. For the first time in her Catholic life, forgiveness did not seem to be enough. She wanted her abuser to be reborn, so she could be reborn. She wanted to trust God to show her the way, but doubts had crept in.

‹‹‹◆›››

Sister Martha was removed from the Prison Outreach program. It devastated her. She had been an advocate for better treatment, fairer sentences, more outside time, exercise, and education. It had become her life, her way of defining herself other than abused kidnap victim. But her disappointment was taken out of her hands. Every inmate but one refused to leave her cell to meet with the sisters. Some were openly crying for Sunny.

Sister Justine came to Sunny's motel room the day before the exiled nun was to return to the convent. "I have to tell you what's happening," Justine said. "Everyone is begging to see you. No prisoner will come out of her cell! Number 4 is stalking the halls like a mad woman, mostly trying to get to that young woman who killed her father."

"I think she'd like me to think she's still in control. Is number 56 safe?" Sunny asked.

"For now," Justine said.

Then some of the women refused to eat. Perfectly good food was thrown away, and negotiators were called in. The prisoners stood arm in arm. Liana raged around them, a lone predator, calling all of Sunny's names. "Rainbow! Baby! You'd better get back here. I'm not through with you yet! You do not get the last word!" The lights inside the prison were left on at night so the inmates could be monitored. Things were spiraling out of control.

After a few days, on her own and against the demands of her order, Sister Martha entered the Nevada State Prison Women's Unit in full habit, her head bowed in prayer. The guards did not bar her way. They clapped as she passed by. The inmates in the yard ran to greet her, and they called out their names: "Sister, I'm Amanda," "Jackie here," "There's Gretchen with her best friend, Jean," "I'm Violet," "I'm Julia," "There's Martina beside Lupe," "Come, Sister, Tyesha needs you and that new girl, Marlene."

Sunny was surrounded by thieves and liars and killers and the few innocents among them. She let them hug her, the first strangers that had ever hugged her. The healing had begun. The kidnapper seemed to be hidden behind the others, her voice suppressed by the sounds of the prisoners thanking Sister Martha for coming back to them. Number 56 grabbed her hands and said, "I'll be all right now, Sister." It was *almost* enough for the Iroquois nun who could not cry.

Then, out of the corner of her eye, she saw a woman fall to the ground clutching her chest. Sister Martha pushed her way through the crowd and went down on her knees beside the struggling woman. It was Liana. The abductor's eyes were frozen with fear. Sunny did not hesitate. She started CPR, putting her mouth on the lips that had bit her and bruised her, filling the lungs of the woman who had denied her fresh air for years and taunted her with blue skies under which she could not play. She pushed back the graying red locks that swirled like snow against her face. "Hold on, damn you!" the nun cried.

Sirens wailed in the distance, but Sunny kept her hands on Liana's chest, maintaining the pulse of the woman who had maimed her childhood heart. "Sunny? ... Sunny," the woman said, a name she had never called the child she had stolen.

The EMTs had to pull the nun away, and Liana lived. She was rushed from the scene, and Sister Martha was given water and a cool place to sit down. She looked around her, dazed and astonished, as though waking from a long sleep, and she spoke in a hoarse whisper, a new light in her dark eyes and a new faith in her battered spirit. She turned toward the retreating ambulance, eerily like a white van in her blurred vision, lifted one hand, and said, "God be with you."